QUEST FOR THE SPARK
BOOK TWO

WRITTEN BY **TOM SNIEGOSKI**
ILLUSTRATED BY **JEFF SMITH**
COLOR BY STEVE HAMAKER

An Imprint of

■ SCHOLASTIC

New York   Toronto   London   Auckland   Sydney   Mexico City   New Delhi   Hong Kong

For Pam Daly,
the best dogsitter a pup could have

Library of Congress Cataloging-in-Publication Data

Sniegoski, Tom.
Quest for the Spark. Book 2 / written by Tom Sniegoski ; illustrated by Jeff
Smith ; color by Steve Hamaker. – 1st ed.
p. cm. – (Bone)
Summary: Twelve-year-old Tom and his cohorts continue their seemingly
impossible quest to find the pieces of the Spark that will save the Dreaming —
and the Waking World — from the evil Nacht.
ISBN 978-0-545-14103-1
ISBN 978-0-545-14104-8 (paperback)
[1. Adventure and adventurers – Fiction. 2. Heroes – Fiction. 3. Dreams –
Fiction. 4. Magic – Fiction. 5. Fantasy. 6. Humorous stories.] I. Smith, Jeff, ill.
II. Hamaker, Steve. III. Title.
PZ7.S68033Que 2012
[Fic] – dc23
2011020281

ACKNOWLEDGMENTS
Cover and interior artwork by Jeff Smith
Text by Tom Sniegoski
Harvestar Family Crest designed by Charles Vess
Color by Steve Hamaker

10 9 8 7 6 5 4 3 2 1   12 13 14 15

First edition, February 2012
Edited by Cassandra Pelham
Book design by Phil Falco
Creative Director: David Saylor

Printed in China   38

Much love and appreciation to my wife for all that she does, and many thanks to Kirby for helping me with the hard parts of this book. Sorry I had to leave out the part about the heroic French bulldog.

Thanks also to Christopher Golden for listening to me complain when the creative juices just weren't flowing, and to Liesa Abrams, James Mignogna, Dave Kraus, Mom and Dad Sniegoski, Mom and Dad Fogg, Pete Donaldson, and Timothy Cole and the Flock of Fury down at Cole's Comics in Lynn.

And once again a HUGE thanks to Jeff and Vijaya for giving me this chance.

Tom

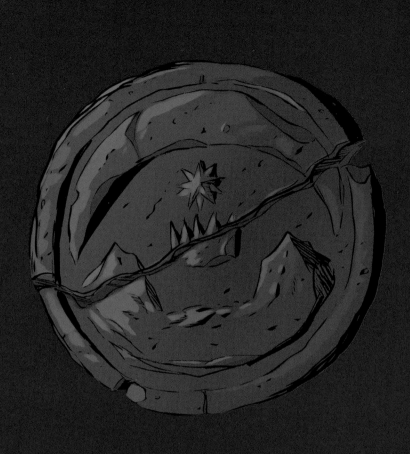

PROLOGUE

The Nacht was feeling stronger.

Stretching his long, muscular neck, the Dragon of darkness purred contentedly as he gazed at the once tranquil landscape about him.

The land of the Dreaming had been lush and green and filled with life, but now . . .

Now it was as it should be.

As it was before the Dreaming existed, when everything was darkness.

Liquid shadow pooled upon the ground, long trailing tendrils of inky black dripping from the branches of once thriving trees. It was as if the Dreaming, and everything within it, had been dipped in the thickest . . . blackest . . . tar.

And the Nacht liked it.

Evil spirits that had chosen to serve him swirled excitedly about his horned head, as the dragon relaxed in a pool that had once been as blue as the summer sky but was now as dark as a moonless night.

"Very nice," one of the spirits hissed.

"I love what you've done with the place," commented another.

The Nacht chuckled, a rumbling sound very much like a savage growl. "It will do for now," he replied. "But there is still much to finish."

"The Dreaming," said a spirit floating in the air before the beast's fearsome face. "It tries to deny you."

"Yes," the Nacht agreed. "It tries . . . but it will fail."

The Dragon raised a huge claw from its ebony bath, and the darkness rippled outward, revealing images from the world beyond the Dreaming.

The Nacht saw the Waking World in all its splendor, but wished to see it drowning in shadow. From the gloom he would reshape it in his own image.

"My power grows," he declared, gazing down into the pool. "First the Dreaming . . . and soon the Waking World as well."

He lifted a muscular limb and dipped a curled talon into the pool, creating another wave of ripples.

The evil spirits flew closer.

"Oh yes, you have been busy," said one as reflections of the damage the Nacht had caused to the Waking World appeared in the shiny liquid. "Your initial attack upon the

Dream Masters and your brother and sister Dragons, leaving them imprisoned in the realm of unconsciousness — very nicely done."

The Nacht grinned, turning his attention to his most valued prizes. In the pool's reflection, he gazed upon the images of Queen Thorn Harvestar and her grandmother, Rose Harvestar — or Gran'ma Ben, he remembered they more often called her — tightly held in the embrace of unnatural sleep. What a nuisance the two had been to the Lord of the Locusts, but to him?

The Nacht grinned. *How could they expect anything but excellence from me?*

"What is this I see?" one of the ghostly shapes asked. It drifted closer to a shimmering image in the pool. "The Dreaming has found a champion?"

The Dragon shifted its powerful bulk in the coal-black waters. "He is just a boy," he said dismissively.

"Yes, but he has gathered others to his cause. . . ."

"And he has found two pieces of the first Spark," added another of the malevolent spirits. "Not bad for just a boy. If he should find all the pieces, then —"

"It will not matter," snapped the Nacht.

The spirits were joined by more of their ghostly kind, all peering at the images of the Dreaming's champions in the inky water.

"They look like a formidable bunch," one of the spirits said cheerfully.

Another floating beside it agreed. "I think the Dreaming has chosen wisely."

With a deafening roar, the Nacht surged up, unfurling his wings and slamming his front legs down, eliminating the images and dispersing the black, oily waters.

"Enough!" he bellowed as the spirits scattered, trying to avoid the Dragon's anger.

One dared to fly closer. "We meant no disrespect, evil one," it apologized. "But the boy and his friends appear to be achieving some measure of success and —"

"And they will fail miserably," the Nacht hollered, blowing the spirit back toward the others hovering a safe distance away.

The Dragon rose up to his full height, his enormous wings slowly fanning the fetid air, his spiked tail swishing back and forth like a pendulum on the pitch-stained ground.

There were new plans to set in motion, plans that would guarantee his success. The Nacht looked out over the Dreaming, and to the Waking World beyond.

And what he saw put a smile upon his monstrous face.

Chapter 1

Tom Elm had always known the Valley was big, but now, as he gazed out over the side of the *Queen of the Sky*, it seemed to stretch on forever.

It also reminded him of just how enormous a task had been entrusted to him.

The magical place called the Dreaming had chosen him to lead a quest to save the Valley from an evil called the Nacht: an evil that threatened to shadow everything in darkness.

"Oh, is that all?" he murmured. Him . . . a twelve-year-old boy and turnip farmer given a job like this. He continued to look out over the Valley as the balloon ship soared above it, and his thoughts drifted to his family — his mother, father, and baby sister, all locked in the grip of an endless sleep.

A chill ran down the boy's spine like an icy finger,

the shaggy hair at the back of his neck prickling to attention. To say that he was afraid was an understatement. He couldn't remember ever being more scared.

This isn't a time for fear, Tom told himself, trying to squelch the flames of anxiety before they could grow too high.

There was too much at stake.

He reached up to grasp the odd, rough stone that hung on a leather thong around his throat, a stone that he once thought lucky because he had found it in the middle of a giant turnip. Tom smiled sadly, remembering simpler times when he didn't have to worry about leading quests and saving the world. Being a turnip farmer suddenly didn't seem so bad.

As it turned out, the stone was actually a fragment of the very first ray of light that had driven back the darkness and nightmares at the beginning of time. Finding it had been the start of his mission for the Dreaming, which was to search out the remaining pieces of the Spark and to make it whole again.

But the evil that threatened the world had plans of its own.

Tom gasped as a vision of four men swam before his mind's eye — the Constable and his deputies, who were possessed by evil spirits serving the Nacht. Tom and his friends had managed to escape them in the *Queen of the Sky*, but something told him that they had not seen the last of those foul creatures, that those who served the Nacht did not give up so easily.

"We're taking her down!" announced a voice from behind, reminding Tom that he wasn't alone in this monumental task. Others had also been chosen.

He turned to watch Percival Bone inside the wheelhouse of the flying ship that the adventurer had built for exploration. Percival quickly worked the various wheels, valves, and levers in order to bring the *Queen of the Sky* closer to earth.

Percival saw that he was being watched, and gave Tom a wave. "This looks to be as good a spot as any," he called out, pointing through the window of the pilot's station at a clearing in the forest below while holding the ship's wheel steady. "Toss out the anchor, and we'll be good to go."

Tom moved, happy to be doing something other than thinking.

A sudden squeal caught his attention, and he looked across the deck. Percival's twin niece and nephew, Abbey and Barclay, and Roderick the raccoon, were cheering and clapping as the Veni Yan priest — Randolf Clearmeadow — performed some kind of magic trick.

Four more who had been chosen to help him with the Dreaming's mission.

The priest reached out and seemed to pluck a coin from

behind Abbey's ear. The little Bone began to laugh hysterically.

"Do I have any money behind my ear?" her brother asked, jumping up and down.

"And me?" Roderick chimed in.

Randolf chuckled. "No, but you can have these," he said, producing three coins from somewhere within his tattered robes, and handing one to each of them. "For the marketplace, perhaps for something sweet."

Abbey's, Barclay's, and Roderick's eyes all grew large.

"Candy," they said in unison.

A Bone explorer with a sky ship, an old Veni Yan warrior priest, a raccoon, and a set of Bone twins were not the most likely choices for a dangerous mission, but the Dreaming moved in mysterious ways.

A twelve-year-old turnip farmer wasn't an obvious choice as leader, either, yet here he was.

And it got even weirder than that.

Tom continued to the far end of the *Queen* toward the ship's anchor, only to find two large, snoring piles of fur. These were the least likely, and strangest members of their group, and they were sleeping on top of the anchor. Tom cleared his throat loudly, hoping to wake them.

The Rat Creatures continued to snore. He saw that one of them — nicknamed Stinky by Barclay Bone — was clutching a dead squirrel to his hairy chest as he slept, like a small child with a doll.

It was certainly a contradiction to see the Rats this way. Rat Creatures, or Hairy Men, as many people called them, were considered to be some of the most dangerous and ruthless creatures in the Valley.

"Hey!" Tom poked Stinky's leg with the toe of his boot. "Wake up!"

The Rat Creature snorted loudly. "Fredrick?" he mumbled. "Where's Fredrick?"

For some reason, Stinky had named his dead squirrel Fredrick, and why he hadn't eaten it yet was another mystery entirely.

"He's right there on your chest," Tom pointed out.

The Rat Creature sighed with relief as he lightly stroked the squirrel's matted fur.

"There you are," Stinky said, kissing the top of the dead rodent's head. The Rat Creature then turned a suspicious eye toward Tom. "What do you want?" he snarled, holding the rotting carcass closer.

"I was wondering if . . ." Tom began, but did not get the chance to finish.

"No, you can't have him!" Stinky screeched as he tried to hide the dead animal behind his back, kicking a clawed foot into the side of his still-sleeping companion. "Wake up! The young mammal wants to take Fredrick! Help!"

Smelly — named by Abbey Bone — awoke with a loud snort.

"Wha? Who?" the furry beast asked, looking around with unfocused eyes.

"The mammal!" Stinky wailed, pointing to Tom. "The mammal wants to take our beloved Fredrick. Do something!"

Tom rolled his eyes. "I don't want to take your squirrel," he said.

Smelly leaned forward to study the boy. "You don't want the squirrel?" he asked suspiciously.

Tom shook his head.

"He doesn't want the squirrel," Smelly said to Stinky.

"How can we be sure he's telling the truth?" Stinky asked, still panicked. He'd brought Fredrick out from hiding and was petting the dead animal furiously.

"Are you sure you're telling the truth?" Smelly asked.

Tom nodded this time.

"He's not lying," Smelly told his friend. "Can I go back to sleep now?"

Stinky was about to answer, when Tom interrupted.

"What I would like is for you two to move," he said.

"See!" Stinky cried. "He wants us to move. First we move and then he snatches away poor Fredrick and —"

"I need the anchor," Tom said, pointing to the floor beneath the Rats. "You two are sitting on it."

Both Rats looked down as they slowly lifted their furry rumps to find the heavy metal anchor beneath them.

"Would you look at that," Smelly said.

"I thought the floor felt a little lumpy," added Stinky, as the two creatures moved aside. "There, there, Fredrick," Stinky cooed, petting the dead rodent. "I won't let the bad mammal take you."

"Do you see what I have to put up with?" Smelly asked the boy as Tom picked up the anchor from beside a coil of thick rope.

The *Queen of the Sky* had come to a stop, and Tom tossed the heavy metal anchor over the side. It hit the grass below with a thud.

"Anchor dropped!" he called out, ignoring Smelly and turning to head back to the wheelhouse. He caught sight of the final member of their party, Lorimar, a supernatural being who had created a physical body for herself by using the plant life of the Valley. The woman stood perfectly still and stared out over the bow, the wind rustling the dark green oak leaves that comprised her hair.

It was Lorimar who had brought Tom the knowledge of the threat that endangered the Dreaming and the Waking World. It was she who told him that the Dreaming had chosen him.

Tom slowly approached her, curious as to what sight held her attention so raptly.

"Lorimar?" he called.

Coming to stand beside her, he looked out and saw only trees and mountains far off in the distance.

But he suspected that she was seeing so much more.

. . .

Lorimar had been reaching out to the worlds beyond the Waking one, desperate to see how bad it had become. It was far worse than she had expected. The Nacht's power was growing, spreading over the lands, and now even the mighty Dragons were held in its monstrous grasp. Lorimar feared for them — and for their quest. She feared for the Valley and the wide world beyond.

Suddenly, there were voices calling to her from across the ether, soft and beckoning from very far away — voices that only she could hear. Momentarily distracted, she concentrated on the faint whispers that begged for her attention.

"Who are you?" she asked, addressing the voices in her mind. *"Where are you?"*

The answer made her want to cry out in shock and surprise.

How is it possible? Her people were no more. . . .

The First Folk had been destroyed when they tried to help the Dragons stop the Lord of the Locusts, who had possessed the flesh of the great Dragon Queen, Mim.

Lorimar had been the only survivor of her kind, or at least, until now, that was what she had believed.

Then, as suddenly as they had sounded, the voices fell silent. Lorimar desperately reached out, searching for them.

But they were indeed gone, and she felt more alone than she had in a very long time.

Tom reached out to touch Lorimar's bark-covered arm.

"Lorimar?" he asked quietly. "Are you all right?"

The tree woman had been standing perfectly still, looking out over the Valley with an intensity that worried him. She shuddered at his touch, her leafy hair rustling as if combed by a sudden wind.

"Tom," she said, turning her dark gaze to him. "What can I do for you?"

"What were you staring at?" He craned his neck to see if he could find anything out of the ordinary.

"I was assessing the danger to the Valley . . . to us," Lorimar replied. "And I'm afraid to say that it is growing."

"Then I guess it's really good that we're on this quest, huh?" Tom asked, the weight of his new responsibility like a sack of rocks around his neck.

"Yes," she agreed, again gazing outward. "But even I am not sure if the threat has not grown too large for us. The Dragons are sleeping now, Tom. The *Dragons*."

Tom didn't know all that much about Dragons, but he knew that they were a powerful force in the Valley, and if *they* were under the Nacht's influence, what chance could he and his small band possibly have?

No, he told himself. He couldn't think like that. He

had to be positive. "Well, the Dragons might be asleep, but we're not, and we're going to stop the Nacht."

She turned her head to him with a rustle of leaves, and he thought he saw the hint of a smile on her wooden features.

"Of course we are," she said. "We must have faith in the power of the Dreaming."

Just then, Percival came around the corner of the wheelhouse, adjusting the strap on a leather bag that he wore over his shoulder.

"There you are," the Bone explorer said. "Are you ready? I've got the kids and the holy man ready to go."

"Are you coming with us?" Tom asked Lorimar.

"Coming where?" she asked.

"We need supplies," Percival answered.

"Yeah," Tom chimed in. "Figured we should probably stock up if we're going on a proper quest. Who knows when we'll get the chance again."

Lorimar gripped the railing in her branchlike hands.

"The Rats," she began. "Will they be accompanying you?"

Tom and Percival turned to see the two Rat Creatures listening.

Stinky waved his dead squirrel at them.

"Not a chance," Percival said.

"No," Tom agreed, shaking his head.

"Then I shall stay here to keep an eye on them," Lorimar said.

"That's a good idea," Percival said. "Still not sure I trust those two a hundred percent."

Tom glanced over to see the Rats glaring at them, and then quickly looking away.

"Fine," he heard Smelly say haughtily.

"We really didn't want to go anyway . . . did we, Fredrick?" Stinky asked his squirrel.

"It's decided, then," Percival said as he turned to leave. "Lorimar stays here with the hair ball twins, and we go get the supplies. Let's shake a leg, Tom."

"Are you sure?" Tom asked her, but she was already back to her place of stillness.

Lost, again, in thought.

Percival, Randolf, the twins, and Roderick had already gone down the rope ladder to the ground below.

Tom hesitated, first looking at the statuelike form of Lorimar still standing at the bow, and then to the Rats. He was a little nervous leaving Lorimar with the two beasts — she seemed far too distracted.

"C'mon, Tom," he heard Percival yell.

"Yeah, Tom, let's get going," added Roderick.

Tom was about to go over the side of the *Queen*, but then stopped. Knowing that he'd be angry with himself if he didn't do this, he left the ladder and walked back toward the Rat Creatures.

"Yes, mammal?" Smelly asked as he stood before them. Stinky was slowly moving his prized dead animal behind his back.

"Just a warning," Tom said, putting on his most serious face. He thought of his father, and how stern he could be at times, and tried to copy the look.

The Rat Creatures watched him with round, shiny eyes.

"You two better behave while we're gone," Tom said, looking from one to the other. "Because if you don't . . ."

He didn't know what to say after, and decided to just end it there.

The Rats were silent, obviously waiting for more, but Tom just turned his back and headed for the ladder. He had thrown one leg over the side of the sky ship, when Smelly finally asked, "If we're not?"

"Yes," Stinky wanted to know as well. "If we should misbehave, what fate will befall us?"

Tom paused, trying to come up with something really horrible to scare them, but he couldn't think of anything right then.

"I really don't want to say," he said. "It's just too horrible to talk about."

The last thing he saw as he scrambled down the ladder was the two Rats clutching each other in fear. He hoped that fear would keep them in line long enough for the others to complete their errands and return to the *Queen*.

"Everything good?" Percival asked as Tom reached the last rung and dropped to the ground.

"Yeah, everything's fine," Tom answered. "So what's our plan?"

Tom felt Randolf's intense stare upon him.

"What's our plan?" the Veni Yan asked, seemingly in good humor, but Tom could tell that there was something else behind the warrior priest's words. "I would assume that you, as *leader* of this . . . quest, would be telling us what the plan is . . . *boy*."

Tom didn't like the way Randolf said the word *boy*. It made him all the more aware of how unlikely it was that the Dreaming would choose him as leader of this strange band, and how much was dependent on him, and them, succeeding.

But the Dreaming *had* chosen him — he couldn't argue with that. He really had only one choice: to lead the best he could.

Tom awkwardly cleared his throat before speaking. "Umm . . . we need supplies before we go on our quest," Tom said. "So we're going to go and get some."

Everyone seemed okay with this, but it didn't change the fact that it felt wrong. He was just a kid, after all . . . and there were adults here.

"Didn't you say there was a village nearby, Randolf?" Tom asked.

The Veni Yan priest stared at him a moment with unreadable eyes, then turned and pointed off into the woods. "If I'm not mistaken, the village of Wolf's Hollow is through those woods," he explained. "I visited their market when still in service to the Veni Yan. We should be able to find everything we need there."

Percival Bone flipped open the flap on his leather satchel and removed a wrinkled piece of paper.

"I took the liberty of making out a shopping list," he said. "First thing we need is potatoes — quite a few bushels if we want to keep the *Queen*'s propellers turning."

"We wouldn't need as many if Abbey and Roderick hadn't used our supply as weapons," Barclay was quick to point out.

"What else were we supposed to throw at the Rat Creatures?" Roderick asked, raising his paws up into the air. "And you were throwing them, too!"

"We shoulda thrown him," Abbey snarled. "Besides, he and Roderick were eating them," she said as she stepped menacingly toward her twin, her hands clenched into fists.

"That's enough of that," Percival said, getting between the perpetually quibbling siblings. He continued to read from the shopping list. "Some dried meats and fruit, maybe some more crackers and —"

"How are we going to pay for this?" Tom interrupted.

Percival looked up.

"Well, I figured we might be able to barter," the Bone said. He was looking inside his satchel again. "I always have a few items on hand from Boneville that the locals might be willing to trade for some goods."

"And I managed to scrounge up a few coins," Randolf added. He reached beneath his robes and produced a small leather pouch. "It's not much, but it's better than nothing." He emptied the contents into the palm of his hand and showed them.

Tom nodded. He was skeptical, but if it was all they had to work with, they'd have to make do.

"All right, then," the leader of the quest said. "Let's go and get ourselves some supplies."

CHAPTER 2

The market in Wolf's Hollow was crowded and filled with the sounds of commerce.

"This must be the place," Percival said as the group emerged from the woods at the outskirts of the bazaar.

Tom had been to many markets before with his family and their turnips, but Wolf's Hollow just might have been the busiest he had ever seen.

His family. Tom thought of them again, locked in the grip of a supernatural sleep by the powers of the Nacht, and he felt his heartbeat quicken. He would give anything to see them awake again.

"The potatoes are probably over there with the produce," Tom said as he fell in behind a man with a wheelbarrow piled precariously with gourds. "The quicker we get this done, the faster we can get back to the ship."

Randolf didn't follow them. Instead he stood looking off in the opposite direction.

"Are you coming, Randolf?" Tom called.

"Go ahead," he replied. "I'll meet up with you. There is something else — something not on Percival's list — that will be required for our journey." Without another word, he was gone, lost in the crowds.

Percival studied his list again. "Hmm, wonder what I could've forgotten?" he mused aloud.

"Guess we'll find out when we see him again," Tom said, reaching out to tug on the explorer's jacket. "First things first: potatoes."

The produce section was enormous. There were fruits and vegetables that Tom had never seen before, and he was certain it all would have been so much more exciting without the looming threat of the Nacht.

With Percival at his side, Tom turned around to make sure that the twins and Roderick were still with them.

The kids were lagging behind, their eyes bulging as they took in all the fabulous sights of the market. They seemed particularly interested in a stand selling delicious-smelling gingerbread candy.

"Can we get some, Uncle Percival?" Barclay asked, clutching the coin Randolf had given him. Abbey nodded eagerly, agreeing with her brother for once.

Percival looked at Tom. "What do you think?" the Bone asked. "Can we trust these monkeys?"

Tom didn't see the harm in it, and besides, the twins and Roderick were only slowing them down.

"Meet us back at the forest path," Tom told them. "And don't get into any mischief."

"Did you hear that?" Percival warned, pointing at each of them in turn. "No mischief."

Abbey, Barclay, and Roderick nodded vigorously, holding their coins in tight little fists, before running off in the direction of the sweets stand.

Randolf Clearmeadow could sense it in the air. A feeling of bad things to come.

It had been a very long time since he'd allowed himself to feel such things, to experience the sensations of the world around him. But since meeting Tom Elm, and deciding that he would join this boy and their group on this supposed quest, things had changed.

Tom said that the Dreaming spoke to him, giving him visions that would lead them to the pieces of the Spark, which would somehow be used as a weapon against a creature of pure darkness called the Nacht — a creature that wished ill for the Valley and all who dwelt within it.

This was a mission of such grave importance entrusted to a boy, three Bones, a forest elemental, two Hairy Men, and a failed Veni Yan warrior priest. Randolf would have laughed if he didn't find it all so disturbing.

He moved through the bustling crowd. Yes, provisions were most certainly a necessity for their travels, but so was what he searched out.

Randolf heard it before he saw it: the clanging of a hammer striking steel, the sound of white-hot metal being forged into instruments of combat.

Weapons.

Randolf zeroed in on the blacksmith's stall, deftly moving between the marketplace patrons. If they were to have any chance of stopping this growing evil — this *Nacht* — there was no doubt in his mind that they would need weapons. If there was anything he had learned in his lifetime, it was that evil did not go down without a fight.

He approached the stall and stopped to admire the many swords, knives, and axes on display.

"Good morning," a heavyset woman with a round, friendly face said.

"Good morning," Randolf replied with a polite bow.

"What may I do for you this day?" she asked with a pleasant smile. "Perhaps you are in need of a new sword, or a dagger?" She removed one of the knives from the display rack and held it out to him, pommel first. He took the offered blade with thanks.

"A fine piece of work," he said, hefting it in his hand. It

was perfectly balanced — excellent for throwing.

Randolf gave the blade back to the woman.

"Perhaps you would like to sample one of our swords?" she suggested. She returned the knife to the display and shifted her attention to the larger weapons.

"No need," Randolf told her. "The quality is impeccable. It would be an honor to acquire from a craftsman who offers such high value."

The woman blushed, briefly turning to look in the direction of a large man in a heavy apron, who toiled at the fiery forge and anvil behind her.

"Wait right here, good priest," she said, momentarily excusing herself. "You should speak with my husband."

Randolf watched as she went to the back of the stall, where the blacksmith worked. The man was hammering a piece of metal on the anvil but paused to listen to his wife, glancing in Randolf's direction as she spoke in excited whispers. Then the blacksmith set his tools down on a wooden table and stepped around the anvil toward the front of his stall.

"Hello," he said in a hearty greeting, pulling thick leather gloves from his hands and shoving them in the belt of his apron. The man had a great barrel chest, a round bald head, and cheeks flushed red from the heat of the forge.

"Good morning," Randolf said, again followed with a bow.

"My wife tells me that you're an admirer of my work," the smith said. He smiled proudly. "I would be honored for you to own one." The blacksmith positioned himself near the display. "What would you like?" he asked.

Randolf first studied the swords, and then the knives.

"I think it would be best if I took them all," the Veni Yan priest said, gesturing toward the rack. "One must be well prepared when undertaking a mission of great importance."

"Very good, sir," the blacksmith said happily, beginning to remove the weaponry. "And might I add that these particular items are some of my finest work."

"Excellent," Randolf said.

"Since you're purchasing multiple items, I'd be happy to give you a deal," the blacksmith offered with a friendly wink.

"A deal," Randolf repeated with a smile, pleased that the man appeared to remember the old ways, and the respect given to the priests of the Veni Yan.

Randolf reached into his robes and removed what he had left of the random bits of coin he'd acquired from storytelling.

"This is what I have," he said, dumping the coins into

the palm of his hand. He held them out toward the black-smith, whose eyes bulged as he saw the amount offered. "It's all yours, along with the gratitude of the Veni Yan and those about to embark on a quest most dangerous," Randolf added.

"Is this some kind of joke?" the blacksmith asked darkly.

"I assure you," Randolf said. "I would not jest about matters so dire."

He watched the blacksmith's expression turn from pleasant to furious. The big man lashed out, slapping the meager coins out of Randolf's hand, sending them flying.

"You've got a lotta nerve," the man snarled. "That wouldn't even pay for the cloth wrapping," he said. His wife nodded vigorously beside him.

"But it's all I have," Randolf said, bending down to pick up the scattered coins. "And the old ways dictate that if a warrior priest is in need of weaponry, it be given to him with the gratitude of those they serve."

"The old ways dictate," the blacksmith repeated with a snarl. "Those are days long gone, priest. Now you have to pay just like everybody else."

Randolf was stunned. At one time, a Veni Yan needed only to ask, and the citizenry would oblige any request.

"We have need of fine weaponry if we are to —"

"Get out of here before I call a constable," the blacksmith said angrily. "I should have known by the looks of you."

The smith's words stung. Randolf looked down and saw himself as others must, wearing the tattered and faded robes of a faith he'd once devoted his life to, but no more.

A crowd had started to form behind him, and Randolf knew it would be wise to move on.

"I meant no insult," he told the smith, as he stepped away from the booth. The blacksmith just glared.

Randolf could feel eyes watching him, could hear the comments as he walked through the crowd.

"What? Did he expect Rolf to give them to him for free?"

"Poor old sod looks like he's had it rough."

Randolf tried not to look at them. He didn't want to see the pity and disgust, where there would have once been, so very long ago, admiration and respect.

It was as if they could see the failure on him, smell the stink of his defeat. How could he have thought, even for the slightest instant, that he could be a protector again? He deserved the life he'd been living these past years, telling stories of the olden days in exchange for just enough money to fill his belly with food and enough cheap ale to forget.

But he never really could forget.

Randolf glanced up to get his bearings, and found himself standing in front of a tent that was set away from the other enclosures. An old woman who was dressed in colorful layers of cloth stood before it, motioning for him to enter with a gnarled, clawlike hand.

He was about to tell her that he did not have time, when he found himself obeying. It was dark and cool inside the tent, but Randolf could see that the old woman now sat behind a table, a wooden cup before her.

"Come in, Veni Yan," she croaked.

"I am Veni Yan no longer," he replied with a slight shake of his head.

The old woman laughed, showing off black, mostly toothless gums.

"Veni Yan no longer?" she said, in a singsong voice. "Once Veni Yan, always Veni Yan," she stated with an enthusiastic nod.

The woman picked up the wooden cup and, placing a skeletal hand over the open top, gave it a hard shake. Randolf watched as small white animal bones spilled onto the tabletop. He had seen things like this before — seers with the ability to divine the future by reading how the bones fell.

The old woman leaned forward, placing her withered face and squinting eyes close to the surface of the table.

"A dark future," she said, her eyes grazing each of the bones. "A dark future for us all, unless . . ."

She looked up at him, her eyes glistening wetly in the darkness of the tent. Randolf waited.

"Unless?" he repeated, hoping to urge her on.

"Unless the mission succeeds," she said, picking up the bones from the table and placing them back inside the cup. "Unless all the threads come together."

Randolf was a bit taken aback. "How . . . ?" he began, stepping toward her as she again shook the bones inside the cup and let them fall onto the table.

"But it cannot succeed without courage," she said, studying the dried animal bones. "Without the courage of all who embark upon this important journey." She lifted her ancient head, her old eyes locking with his. "Without

your courage," she added, stressing the importance of the meaning in her foreboding words.

"It has been many years since the spirit of courage coursed through these limbs," Randolf said, looking at his hands.

The fortune-teller seemed not to be listening. She swiped her hand across the surface of the table, collecting all the bones, and dropped them noisily into the cup.

"The Valley needs you, Veni Yan," she said, shaking the bones even more forcefully. "The Dragons need you."

Randolf gasped, stunned by this revelation.

"The Dragons?"

The old woman seemed to be in a kind of trance as she again prepared to roll the bones. "They sleep and cannot awaken . . . held in the grip of something evil."

The bones bounced upon the table, and the fortune-teller studied where they lay. Then she turned her gaze upon him again, her eyes slowly coming into focus.

"The Valley needs you to forgive yourself, and to start living again," she said, holding out her hand for payment. "We're done here, Veni Yan."

"But I never intended to . . ." Randolf started to object, not wanting his fortune told, and certainly not if he had to pay. But he knew that it was the right thing. She had read the bones for him.

With a heavy sigh, he removed the coins that he had

hoped would provide weaponry, and dropped them into the center of the old woman's leathery palm.

"Take them," he told her. "It's all I have."

She counted the money, poking the coins with a long-nailed finger.

"You are a man of honor," she said. "A man of the old ways."

"Days long gone, I'm afraid," he said, remembering what had occurred at the blacksmith's stand.

"My husband was very much like you," the old woman said with a sad smile. "And a priest of the faith."

"He was Veni Yan?" Randolf asked.

She nodded. "He was."

"And is he still with us?"

She sadly shook her head. "Only in my memory. He was taken by the Hairy Men," she explained. "But not before sending many of them to their deaths."

"I'm sure he served the faith well," Randolf said, feeling an urge to leave this place. He was about to say his good-byes when she spoke again.

"My husband left me only with my memories of him, and these," she said as she turned in her chair, and picked up something wrapped in a thick, dusty blanket.

She sat upright and placed the bundle on the table before her.

Randolf stared as her old hands unwrapped the

package. "His weapons," he whispered, gazing down at a sword, short sword, and dagger.

The fortune-teller nodded. "They have been with me since his passing, collecting dust. I knew there was a reason other than his memory that I kept them. Something told me that there would come a time when they would be needed again."

"I could never take another man's weapons," Randolf protested.

"He has no need of them," the woman said. "Think of them as part of my reading." She pushed the items closer to the table's edge. "Think of them as your fortune . . . as part of your future."

Randolf knew that it would be an insult to refuse her. He reached down, first picking up the sword. It felt right in his hand, as if made for his grip. It had some minor patches of rust that needed tending, but it was a good weapon. The short sword felt just as comfortable, and the knife was as good — if not better — than the one he already carried.

"I thank you," Randolf said. Maybe the old ways weren't quite as dead as he believed.

The old woman bowed her head.

"If the bones are correct," she said, "and there are indeed dark times on the horizon, then I should be thanking you, for you are to embark upon a quest for the sake of us all."

· · ·

Tom held his breath, waiting for the farmer's response.

The tall, older man, with a piece of straw sticking from a corner of his mouth, studied the brightly colored cube with drawings of happy cows painted on all of its sides.

"Turn it over," Percival ordered excitedly.

The old farmer did as he was told.

"Moooooooooooooooooooooooooooooooooo!" the cow box said.

The farmer seemed a little surprised and held the box away from him before turning it over again.

"Moooooooooooooooooooooooooooooooooo!" the box said again.

Percival laughed, rubbing his chubby white hands together. "What do you think of that?" he asked happily. "Pretty clever, eh?"

Tom studied the old-timer's face, hoping for the best. They really needed those potatoes.

"Nope," the farmer said, handing the box back to the Bone. "Don't need a box that makes cow noises." The straw in his mouth moved from one side to the other. "I got cows for that."

"Drat," Percival said, taking back the box and returning it to his bag. "Well, if you don't want that, how about . . ."

Tom looked over the Bone's shoulder, trying to see what else he might have in the bag. Percival removed what looked to be a stack of small cards and started to go through them.

"Ah, here we go. Here's a whole set of Famous Bones of Boneville trading cards," he said, looking at each picture. "We got George Washingbone, Napoleon Boneapart, Daniel Bone, Justin Beibone . . . we got 'em all."

He presented them to the farmer, but the man shook his head as he stifled a yawn.

"Think it might be time to pack up my spuds and get going," he said, making a move toward the wooden crate filled with potatoes.

"Wait!" Tom cried anxiously. "Percival was just saving the best for last," he said, not at all sure what he was doing.

The Bone explorer looked at him. "I was?" he asked cautiously.

Tom widened his eyes and slowly nodded.

"I was!" Percival exclaimed. "I knew you were a man of amazing taste, so I was saving this special item just for you and . . ."

He began to paw through the bag again.

Tom smiled at the farmer. "You're really gonna like this," he said. "Isn't he, Percival?"

"Yeah," said the Bone, furiously searching. "Yeah . . . if only I could see what's at the bottom of this darn bag," he muttered.

He reached up, removed a shiny metal object from his shirt pocket, and, clicking a button at its end, sent a beam of light down into the bag.

Tom gasped, as did the farmer.

Percival looked up. "What?" he asked. "Never seen one of these before?" he asked, holding out the metal object. "It's a flashlight." He clicked the light off and handed it over to the curious farmer. "It's like a candle, but it won't burn you."

"That's amazing," Tom said.

"Yeah," Percival agreed. "I guess it is."

The farmer studied the cylinder, looking into the part where the light had come from.

"Push that button on the end," Percival instructed.

The farmer turned the strange object around, and found the button. Tentatively he pushed it, turning on the beam of light. He gasped again, pointing the light in all different directions. "What do you call this again?"

"It's a flashlight," the Bone explorer said.

"Flashlight," the farmer repeated, as if the word were magic.

"And it can be yours for this crate of potatoes," Tom suddenly said.

Percival looked at him, horrified. "But it's my only one." The Bone looked back to the farmer, who was now shining the beam onto the palm of his hand and grinning with wonder.

"All right, fine," the Bone agreed. "But you've got to throw in some apples."

Tom approached the farmer, who was still playing with the flashlight.

"So, do we have a deal?" he asked.

The old man pulled his attention away from the incredible device. With a smile, he stuck out a dirty hand.

And the two shook on it.

Roderick licked the last of the honey-ginger candy from his paws, wishing that he had some more.

"That was the best candy I ever had," the raccoon said to his two friends.

Abbey was still working on her stick of candy, eating it slowly to make it last. Barclay had finished his even quicker than Roderick, and was now eyeing what was left of his sister's treat.

"I think my piece was smaller than everybody else's," Barclay complained.

"It wasn't smaller," Abbey said around her candy. "You're just a pig and wolfed it down before you could enjoy it."

"No, sir," Barclay protested. "You got the biggest piece and you should share what you have left with the two of us. Right, Roderick?"

"I don't know about that," Roderick said. "I'm feeling kinda guilty that I had any candy to begin with."

"Guilty?" Barclay asked in dismay. "For what?"

The raccoon shrugged his little shoulders. "I don't know, it's just that we coulda put our coins toward provisions for the quest instead of getting candy."

"I didn't even think of that," Barclay said with a shake of his head.

"Me, neither," Abbey said, staring at the last of her honey-ginger candy. "I don't even want this now."

The three friends fell silent.

After a few moments, Abbey took what was left of her candy and broke it into three smaller pieces. She handed one to Roderick, one to her brother, and kept the last for herself.

"No sense in letting perfectly good candy go to waste," she said.

Roderick nibbled on his piece, while Barclay gobbled his up.

"I feel awful," Abbey said.

"It was good candy, though," Barclay replied, licking the tips of his fingers one at a time.

They all nodded silently.

"We should do something for the quest," Roderick said suddenly.

"Like what?" Barclay asked.

The raccoon pulled on the fur of his chin as he thought.

"I got it!" he cried out. "We can help with the provisions."

"What do you mean, like food and stuff?" Barclay asked. "Hate to remind you, but we spent our money on the candy."

"Yeah, how are we gonna get anything to eat without any money or stuff to trade?" Abbey wanted to know.

"We won't need any of that," the raccoon said. He scampered across to an overturned tree stump, which was covered in strangely shaped mushrooms. "We can get food for free right here." He pointed to the odd growths on the stump.

The twins' faces twisted up in confusion.

"I think you've eaten too much candy," Barclay said.

"Yeah, it's made you plumb loco," Abbey agreed, moving a finger in a circular motion at the side of her head.

"Don't you get it?" Roderick asked. "These mushrooms . . . you can eat them."

"They look disgusting," Abbey commented, scrunching up her nose.

Barclay stepped in for a closer look. "How do you know we can eat them?"

"Remember, I used to live in the wild before I moved in with Tom and his family. I ate all kinds of stuff. It doesn't matter how it looks," the raccoon said, his eyes scanning the area. "Lots of stuff around here can be eaten." He darted over to a dark green bush heavy with fat, red berries. "These are called rook berries, on account of the rooks really loving them. They're kinda sour, but not bad."

The twins studied the bush, and Barclay reached out to poke one of the fat growths.

"And this over here," said the raccoon, presenting an area of tall, green grass. "This stuff isn't bad once you chew it for a while." He moved his paws over the thin blades as the twins looked on. "Kinda like spinach, only sweeter."

He parted the long grass to see what might be on the other side — and found himself looking into a pair of large, bulbous eyes.

"Hmm, what the heck are these?" he asked aloud, moving closer for a better look.

The twins were standing far enough back that they could see exactly what had been exposed in the shadowy patch behind the grass, and Abbey squealed a warning. "Roderick, look out!"

The Rat Creature's head shot out from the darkness, its huge mouth open wide as it tried to chomp down on the little raccoon.

Roderick jumped back just as the creature's jaws snapped closed like a bear trap. "Eeeeek!" he cried, as he quickly scurried away to join the twins.

They were all too stunned to speak, watching with terror-filled eyes as the Rat Creature emerged from its hiding place to reveal yet another surprise.

A man was riding atop the creature's back, holding on

to thick handfuls of the Rat's fur like reins.

"Well, hello, children," the man said, his eyes so big and black that it was as if his head were filled with night. "Aren't you the cutest things."

And then three more Rat Creatures with humans riding upon their backs stepped out from the shadows.

"Cute enough to eat," said the Rat that had emerged first. It stared hungrily at Roderick and the twins as its thick, pink tongue slid across a row of razor-sharp teeth.

CHAPTER 3

The evil spirit living inside the body of Constable Roarke was suddenly very happy.

Just goes to show you, he thought as he sat astride the Rat Creature — King Agak, no less — and looked at the two children and the raccoon. *You never know what you'll find when you poke around in the woods.*

He and three others of his kind had been given the task of stopping the Dreaming's champions, to prevent them from challenging the supremacy of their lord and master, the great and powerful Nacht.

But the evil spirits, so far, had been less than successful.

First they had failed to persuade the boy to ignore the Dreaming's request to take up its cause, and then they had failed to prevent the gathering of those who would help the boy carry out his mission.

Minor setbacks, thought the Constable, as he tried to

keep his balance atop the humped back of the Rat King. He had no doubt that they would eventually track down the boy and his companions, and stop their infernal quest.

Especially now that the spirits had allied themselves with the Rat Creatures. The Hairy Men had excellent tracking skills and were actually already hunting two of their own for some act of betrayal — two of their own who had taken up with the boy and his rabble.

And now they had found the children and the raccoon.

"You three wouldn't happen to know the whereabouts of a boy named Tom Elm, would you?" the Constable asked.

"Who wants to know?" the Bone boy challenged, puffing out his chest.

The Constable chuckled. "Well, I do," he said. "And so do my friends." He gestured to his three deputies sitting astride their Rat Creature mounts. They, too, were amused by the little Bone's show of defiance.

"Tom Elm?" the little girl chimed in. "Tom Elm . . ." she said again. "Nope, never heard of him. . . . Nice talking to you, mister." She grabbed at Barclay and Roderick. "C'mon, fellas. Uncle Percival's gonna be mad if we're late."

"Wait," the Constable ordered, as he prepared to dismount. "As a man of the law," he continued, "I wish to question you about an escaped fugitive . . . a Veni Yan priest who —"

And then the unthinkable happened. King Agak, who had behaved quite well until this point, surged forward, causing the Constable to fall backward to the ground.

"Get back here!" the Rat King screeched, baring his razor-sharp teeth as he lunged for the children and the raccoon.

The three screamed, turned tail, and ran off in different directions into the surrounding woods. Agak started in pursuit, but the Constable reached out and grabbed hold of one of the Creature's back legs.

King Agak hissed and bared his teeth at the Constable. The other Rats were agitated now.

"We need them alive," the Constable said in the ancient language of the Rats, still holding the Rat King's leg in a powerful grip.

"I'm starving," Agak roared.

"We need them to find the boy," the Constable explained calmly.

"I'll only eat one of them," Agak said, trying to yank his leg free.

"You'll eat none of them," the Constable corrected.

The Rat King looked as though he'd been slapped.

"How dare you tell me —"

"You'll eat none of them until we find the ones we're looking for," the Constable interrupted.

"And when we find them?" Agak questioned.

"Then they can all be eaten," the Constable answered, a large smile forming upon his lips.

A smile almost as wide as the Rat Creature King's.

The box of potatoes was heavy, but Tom managed. He'd carried many a crate of turnips over the years, and this was only a little bit heavier than those.

"So, we did pretty good, don't you think?" he asked Percival, who was walking beside him with a sack of apples slung over a shoulder.

"Yep, not bad," the Bone explorer said. "Those spuds should keep us moving through the air for a good long time, and all it cost us was a little haggling time and an old flashlight. Not bad at all."

They were heading through the market, back toward the edge of the woods to meet the others, when they caught sight of a figure walking in their direction.

"Here comes Randolf," Percival said.

As if on cue, the figure looked up and started to wave.

"What's he carrying?" Tom asked, squinting. It looked like something wrapped in an old blanket.

"I was just about to ask the same thing," Percival said, walking faster.

"Hey, wait for me," Tom called out, trying to keep up while lugging the potatoes.

Randolf seemed strangely enthusiastic — the first time

Tom could remember seeing the man genuinely excited about anything.

"What's this?" Percival was asking as Tom joined them.

"If I hadn't stopped believing in such things," Randolf said, "I would say that a gift has been bestowed upon us by a higher power."

The warrior set the blanket on the ground and opened it to expose the contents.

"A higher power gave you an old sword?" the Bone explorer asked.

Tom set the potatoes down and came for a look. "Looks like there's a short sword and dagger, too," he observed.

"They are for the quest," Randolf said. "If the Nacht is as savage as you say, then he will stop at nothing to keep us from defeating him. These should help us."

Tom felt his stomach tighten. At that moment, the dangers of the quest became much more real.

"Wouldn't want to mess with us now," Percival said. He picked up the short sword and chopped the air before clumsily dropping the blade, narrowly missing his foot with its pointed tip.

"Careful, Bone," Randolf warned as he reached down to retrieve the sword. "One must be trained before it can be put to proper use."

"Yeah, I guess," Percival agreed. "Could probably benefit from some lessons on how not to cut off my own foot."

Randolf returned the short sword to the blanket and started wrapping the bundle back up again. Tom bent down to retrieve his potatoes.

"We should get going," Tom said. "Wouldn't want Abbey, Barclay, and Roderick getting impatient. Who knows what kind of trouble they could get into."

A high-pitched scream cut through the air.

"What the . . ." Percival began, as they all looked to see Abbey, Barclay, and Roderick running from the woods.

Just as the Rat Creatures, with the Constable and his three deputies riding atop them, exploded from the underbrush in hot pursuit.

The marketplace went wild as people cried out and tried to run away, their newly purchased goods flying out of their hands.

Tom stayed where he was as if rooted to the spot. He saw everything in slow motion — each and every detail. He watched as Barclay, Abbey, and Roderick ran as fast as their little legs could carry them, watched as the Constable and his men pushed their hairy, monstrous steeds after them, while more Rat Creatures, riderless, swarmed from the forest.

Two farmers, one with a pitchfork and another with a flaming torch, ran at the beasts, but the Rat Creature ridden by the Constable reared up and slashed at the men with his front claws. The men screamed, their fear getting the better of them, as they dropped their weapons and ran away to join the panicking crowds.

But they did not escape — none of the market folk did.

Tom watched in horror as something seeped up from the ground while the people ran about in chaos. At first he thought it was a trick of his eyes but then realized what he was seeing.

A kind of black smoke was snaking up from the ground, seemingly drawn to the townspeople. It coiled through the air, and as it encircled each of them, one by one they fell to the ground, asleep.

Tom remembered his parents and little sister, as well as the village where they'd first rescued Randolf. The Nacht's evil was spreading.

A screaming Abbey, Barclay, and Roderick reached Percival and Randolf, all three of them talking at once, trying to explain that they hadn't done anything wrong.

But there was no time for that now.

"Get the children to safety!" Randolf screamed.

Percival gathered up the twins and raccoon, ushering them quickly away. The Bone explorer's eyes locked onto Tom's.

"Are you coming?"

Tom felt his legs begin to move. A tiny voice in his mind was screaming for him to run, but then something

stopped him. The Spark around his neck grew warm, the heat spreading through his body as if he were standing in a beam of hot August sun.

"You go," Tom ordered. "I'm staying here."

He saw the look of surprise in Percival's eyes, but the Bone didn't hesitate. He grabbed the kids and hauled them away as fast as he could. Tom turned back to see that Randolf had taken the sword from the blanket and was advancing toward the Rats.

Tom paused, not sure if he had made the right choice, but that doubt was cast aside when he felt the pulsing warmth of the fragment of Spark dangling around his neck. If he was ever going to be a leader, these were the kinds of things — no matter how terrifying — he would have to do. Without another thought, Tom reached into the blanket on the ground and withdrew the rusty short sword and dagger, and then ran to stand at Randolf's side.

"Get away from here," the Veni Yan said, not taking his gaze from the advancing beasts. "You're far from ready for this, boy."

"I'm going to need to be ready sometime," Tom said, doing everything he could to keep his growing fear under control. "And now looks to be as good a time as any."

CHAPTER

The two Rats were hot on Percival's heels as he raced through the marketplace. He could hear them at his back, snorting and growling, their distinctive stink — like a wet dog rolled in garbage — wafting in the air.

Abbey, Barclay, and Roderick ran ahead of him while the market people ran all around, some screaming at the sight of the filthy beasts, others falling to the ground, fast asleep. The Bone adventurer's eye caught what looked to be a sort of black smoke seeping up from the ground. He didn't know what it was, but it couldn't be good. They needed to get out of there and back to the *Queen* as quickly as possible.

The Rats were close, real close. Their feet pounded the dirt floor, the vibration making Percival's legs tingle.

"Bang a left!" he screamed out to the kids.

Abbey and Barclay took the sharp corner around a stall

selling cheese products, but Roderick went the other way.

"The other left!" Percival cried out, shifting slightly to snag the raccoon by the tail. Roderick yelped as he was flung onto the right course.

"I always have trouble with that," the little raccoon said breathlessly.

The Rats were nipping at their heels, and Percival didn't know how much longer they could keep this up. Ahead, he saw a row of tents and stalls. Maybe . . . just maybe . . . they might be able to duck inside. It was worth a try.

"Inside!" he yelled to the twins as they passed a booth selling woven blankets. An idea had popped into his head. "Keep going," he ordered the raccoon.

Then the Bone adventurer grabbed one of the blankets from the booth, spun around, and, with a grunt, hurled it up and over the heads of the approaching Rats.

"That oughta slow you down some," he said, stopping for a moment to watch as the Rat Creatures stumbled, growling and roaring as they tried to rip off the covering.

Percival turned and caught sight of Roderick and the twins slipping inside a large, blue tent. He quickened his pace to join them, hoping the Rats wouldn't free them- selves before he got there.

It was dark inside the tent and he could hear the kids bumping into things.

"Shhhhhh!" he said, dropping to the floor behind what

looked to be a large wooden table. He could just make out Abbey and Barclay to his right, their eyes wide and white in the darkness. A warm body pressed to his leg told him that Roderick was close by. They waited for what seemed like an eternity, but the Rats didn't appear, and Percival began to think that maybe their luck had changed.

Not.

One of the Rats suddenly tore away the flap of the tent with a growl, sticking its large, shaggy head inside as sunlight streamed in — revealing Roderick and the Bones behind the table.

But the light also showed Percival that the table was piled high with stacks of cast-iron frying pans. In fact, the whole tent was filled with all kinds of cooking materials, from pots and pans to spoons and spatulas.

The Rat Creature smiled sadistically before it pounced.

Percival snatched up the largest of the frying pans before him and smashed it, as hard as he could, into the face of the attacking Rat. The sound of cast iron hitting furry face was one of the sweetest sounds the Bone adventurer had ever heard.

"Take that, you filthy animal," he cried as the Rat Creature stumbled back, bits of shattered teeth raining from its mouth like confetti. It collapsed to the ground in a heap. The Bone carefully approached the Rat, poking it with his boot to be sure it wasn't bluffing. He was about to turn back to the kids when a second Rat Creature stuck its monstrous face into the tent.

Percival jumped back and raised his frying pan, readying for battle, when he heard a terrifying noise behind him. He whipped around and saw Abbey, Barclay, and Roderick, all wearing cooking pots atop their heads, screaming and waving spatulas and giant serving spoons as if they were residents of Crazy Town. The kids charged the startled Rat Creature, driving him back through the entrance to the tent.

Randolf Clearmeadow, with Tom at his side, hefted his sword and prepared to strike at the advancing Rat Creatures and the agents of the Nacht.

How many times had he done this? How many times had he hurled himself into the heat of battle against these Hairy Men without a care for his own safety? At one time he'd stupidly believed himself invincible and had always emerged from battle victorious . . . until the night his wife and child were taken by the Rats, and he had suffered a fate more horrible than death.

The Veni Yan warrior priest was finally killed by his enemies, and there wasn't a mark upon his body.

The Rats had killed his heart. And now the Dreaming

supposedly had need of him again, a tired and beaten wreck of a man called back into service on a quest to save the Valley.

A quest to be led by a mere boy, Randolf thought as he stood in the marketplace with the Rat Creature bearing down upon him, opening wide its mouth of many teeth.

Tom chanced a quick glance to his side, his legs trembling so hard that he was certain he would fall. The priest stood, staring straight ahead, his sword raised as the lead Rat Creature with the Constable riding on his back galloped closer.

What am I supposed to do? the boy wondered feverishly. *This is crazy. I don't know anything about fighting!*

"You really think you're ready for this, boy?" the Veni Yan asked, eyes fixed to the quickly approaching threat.

"No," Tom answered honestly, hoping that he didn't sound as terrified as he felt. "But if the Dreaming has chosen me, I'm going to have to be."

"The Dreaming," Randolf repeated. "Up to her old tricks again."

Tom didn't understand what he meant, but he didn't say anything.

"Pay attention, quest leader," he heard Randolf say, as the Veni Yan priest launched himself toward their attackers. "You might learn something."

. . .

Tom watched, and did learn.

He learned how sometimes one needed to charge forward even when the odds looked grim. He learned to stare in the eye the thing that most terrified him, and to deny its power.

He learned of bravery.

"Stay close to me, boy," Randolf called out as more beasts stalked from the forest and cautiously tried to encircle them. "Is our back clear?"

Tom turned quickly to look. At the moment it was.

"Yes," he said, watching as the Rat King slashed out, its claws just missing the warrior priest.

There were more Rats now, and they were getting bolder.

"Surrender to us," the Constable said from atop his abominable steed. "Surrender to us and all will —"

"Run!" Randolf commanded sharply. He was already on the move, expecting that Tom would be right behind him.

And Tom did not care to disappoint.

They ran behind some of the market tents. The grounds there were muddy and slowed them down, and the Rats were only temporarily surprised by their sudden departure.

The Veni Yan stopped. "Go," he ordered again. "Catch up with the others. I will meet you if I can."

The monsters were coming at them again — a mass of

fur, claws, and fangs. Even if Randolf was willing to sacrifice his life so that Tom could get a head start back to the sky ship, Tom knew there was a chance he still wouldn't make it. Now was the time to show the Veni Yan what the priest's example of bravery had taught him.

Tom's eyes darted around, looking for anything that could delay the beasts and buy him some additional time. Nearby was a booth that sold hot snacks, a brazier of burning coals used to roast chestnuts and popcorn that made the air above it shimmer in its heat.

Tom had an idea, and he started moving before he could give himself the chance to consider whether it was good or not. He ran toward the brazier, pulling the sleeves of his smock down around his hands.

"What are you doing?" Randolf yelled, crouched and ready for combat. "Get out of here before —"

Tom reached for the metal container and flipped it. Hot coals spilled into the Rat Creatures' path. Sparks like a thousand fireflies leaped into the air as the dried leaves and grass of the market grounds ignited, creating a burning wall that drove the hissing beasts and their riders back.

"Now we can both run," Tom said, tugging on the Veni Yan's arm and leading the way.

CHAPTER 5

The voices of her people softly called to her, and Lorimar strained to understand them.

"Help us," they cried so sadly that she was nearly overcome with emotion.

"How is this possible?" she asked.

"We live," the voices of the First Folk replied.

Lorimar desperately reached out with her mind. *"Where are you?"* she asked. *"Tell me so I can help you."*

The voices fell silent, and Lorimar was suddenly afraid. All this time, she had thought herself the only one of her people left. What if she wasn't able to find them?

"Are you still there?" she asked. "Please, where are you?"

Lorimar let her thoughts roam beyond the Valley, and suddenly her mind was filled with the vision of a place lovely and green. She could feel the impression of a cooling breeze upon her senses. She knew this place, but it had been taken from her, like her people, and corrupted by darkness.

As if on cue, shadows billowed, like ink injected into water. They circled the trees and flowers, trying to constrict the green within their shadowy grip.

But the special place remained, a bubble of paradise trapped in a sea of darkness.

"*Here,*" the voices of the First Folk cried. "*We are here.*"

Then as quickly as the image had come, it was gone, leaving Lorimar with a desperate longing for what she had thought was lost forever.

"I'm starving," Stinky said, his hungry gaze on his sleeping comrade.

"*Snork!*" Smelly responded, smacking his lips, deep in slumber.

"Did you hear me?" Stinky asked as he slapped the side of his friend's head.

Smelly awoke with a snarl on his lips. "What now?" he snapped.

"I said I'm hungry." Stinky pouted.

"Go to sleep and you won't know it." Smelly started to close his eyes again, but Stinky wasn't having any.

"I can't," he said. "My stomach is making so much noise. It's keeping me awake."

"Then eat the squirrel," Smelly suggested. "There won't be much left of him soon anyway."

"Eat Fredrick?" Stinky was horrified. "I would rather die."

Smelly rose up on his powerful, furry haunches, turned his back, and settled back down to return to sleep.

"Aren't you hungry?" Stinky asked.

Smelly tried to ignore him, but . . .

Glurrgle.

"That wasn't my stomach," Stinky said. "You *are* hungry!"

"I am not," Smelly emphatically denied.

Glurrble bloop!

"Your stomach begs to differ," Stinky pointed out. "And Fredrick thinks you're hungry, too. Don't you, Fredrick?"

Smelly spun around with a snarl. "And what if I am?" he asked. "If we're not going to eat that squirrel . . ."

Stinky screeched, nuzzling the rotting corpse of the squirrel to his throat.

"Well?" Smelly prompted. *Gloorbb! Blapp!* his stomach echoed.

Stinky tapped Fredrick's skull against his lower lip, deep in thought. Then he turned to stare across the deck at a figure standing perfectly still.

Lorimar.

"How about her?" Stinky shrugged.

"Her?" Smelly asked. "But we promised the mammal boy we'd behave while he was gone."

They both looked at Lorimar now, who was still gazing out over the side of the sky ship.

"When have we ever kept a promise?" Stinky asked. "Besides, if they really wanted us to behave, they should have left us something to eat."

"I guess," Smelly said. "But she doesn't look like she'll taste very good. Too many leaves and branches . . . You know I'm not much for vegetables."

Stinky had to agree. "You might be right. On the other hand, once we gnaw through the bark, there might be a delicious meaty center."

"Mmmmm." Smelly was beginning to look at Lorimar in a completely different light. "Well, I'm game if you are," he said. "How should we do this?"

"She seems pretty out of it," Stinky said, watching the tree woman.

"Maybe we could just sneak up on her?" Smelly suggested.

"An excellent idea," Stinky said. "We'll use our natural stealth and cunning." He dropped down low to the deck and began to stalk toward their unsuspecting prey. "Follow me," he urged his friend. "Our bellies will be full in no time."

The voices of Lorimar's people remained silent, no matter how hard she tried to rouse them.

"Are you there?" She reached out with the tendrils of her consciousness, attempting to travel even farther than before. *"Can you hear me? Please, answer . . . please . . ."*

But still the First Folk said nothing.

Lorimar stood quietly at the rail of the *Queen of the Sky* for quite some time, allowing the feelers of her mind to stretch out over the Valley and into the ether beyond. She would not give up now — she had to find them.

"Lorimar!"

The voice filled her heart with joy.

"Yes, yes, I hear you," she said with her mind, before realizing that her name had been spoken aloud and carried by the wind.

"Lorimar, we could use some help here!"

The forest woman pulled back her psychic tendrils, returning to the here and now, and to the deck of the *Queen of the Sky.*

"Lorimar, can you hear me?"

It was Tom, and his voice was rife with panic.

Stinky could almost taste the tree woman.

He was hoping that he was right, that beneath her

bark would be a delicious, soft meat that would silence the grumbles of his empty belly.

"This is how it's done, Fredrick," the Rat whispered to the dead squirrel he still clutched in one of his claws.

"Quiet," Smelly warned, at his back. "We don't want to —"

"Lorimar!" cried a vaguely familiar voice from somewhere nearby.

"Is that the mammal boy?" Stinky asked.

"Lorimar, we could use some help here!" cried the boy's voice. It was coming from below the sky ship.

Stinky paused, turning slightly and cocking one of his pointed ears as he listened. "I believe it is."

"Lorimar, can you hear me?" Tom called, his cries closer now.

"They're back too soon," Stinky growled. "We'd better act fast."

He rose up on his furry haunches just as Lorimar spun around, the thick leafy branches on her head slashing his face and poking his eyes.

"EEEEYAAARRRGH!" Stinky bellowed as he jumped back, arms flailing to protect his face.

Smelly had been standing directly behind his comrade, and when Stinky violently bumped into him, both went stumbling backward. The collision sent Fredrick flying from Stinky's clutches, up into the air, then falling to the deck of the *Queen*. Smelly tried to stop but he stepped on Fredrick's squishy body, sending his clawed foot sliding out from beneath him.

As Smelly fell, he dragged Stinky on top of him, and the two became a rolling ball of screeching Rat Creature fury, on a collision course with the ship's side.

Lorimar could only watch, dumbfounded, as the two Rat Creatures rolled across the deck of the *Queen*, their momentum sending the squealing fur balls over the side of the ship.

She rushed to the other side of the deck and peered over the edge of the rail, to find the Rats lying stunned on the ground below.

"Lorimar!"

She heard her name screamed from across the clearing and turned her eyes to the edge of the woods. What she saw then would have made her blood — if she'd had any — turn to ice.

Tom and the others were running out of the woods, Rat Creatures and servants of the Nacht in close pursuit.

Lorimar was about to act, but suddenly the voices of the First Folk clouded her mind, making it hard for her to concentrate. They, too, were begging for her help.

Desperately, she looked down at the two Rat Creatures on the ground. It had to be up to them now. The lives of Tom and the others were in their claws.

Stinky lay on the ground, visions of soft, juicy animals dancing around his head.

"I'll have one of those, and one of those, and one of those . . ." he slurred as he watched the imaginary critters dance before his bleary eyes.

Smelly was quicker to recover, moaning in pain as he climbed to his feet. He watched his comrade plucking at the air. "What are you doing?"

"I'm picking my meal," Stinky said happily. "Such a delicious selection . . . hello, little piggy!"

Smelly rubbed his sore backside. "You landed on your head again, didn't you?"

"Only a little," Stinky said, reaching up to touch the side of his furry skull. "It hurts a little here. Think I'll have some nice suckling pig and then lie down for a nap."

"You'll do nothing of the sort." Smelly yanked his friend to his feet. "We have other things to worry about."

He pointed to the edge of the clearing, where the shapes of Tom Elm, Randolf, Percival, the twins, and Roderick the raccoon suddenly emerged from the line of trees. They were running.

"Hello, fellas!" Stinky hollered with a wave, finding it a bit difficult not to sway.

And then the Rats realized the group was being chased.

"King Agak!" Smelly squeaked, grabbing hold of Stinky's arm.

The two held each other tightly in fear.

"What are we going to do?" Smelly asked.

"Perhaps we should hide?" Stinky suggested.

"That's a good idea," Smelly said, watching as the mammals and the Rats drew closer.

"Wait, what about Fredrick?" Stinky suddenly asked.

"He can take care of himself," Smelly answered.

"How dare you?" Stinky said in horror. "After all he's given you."

"All he's given me is pain and misery, which is something, seeing as how he's nothing but a dead squirrel. Now let's get out of here."

"I don't know you anymore," Stinky said with a sad shake of his head. Then he turned toward the *Queen*, reaching for the rope ladder that still hung from her side. "First we'll get Fredrick, then we'll hide from the King, and —"

"You two!" a woman's voice bellowed from above.

Both Stinky and Smelly looked up to see the plant woman — the cause of their current predicament — peering at them over the side of the ship.

"We're coming up!" Stinky said, grabbing hold of the ladder with a clawed hand.

"You'll do no such thing," Lorimar commanded.

"But we have to get Fredrick!" Stinky screeched, on the verge of panic.

"If you ever want to see your dead squirrel again, you will go to the aid of your comrades." She pointed a long, branchlike finger in the direction of the group racing across the clearing.

Stinky and Smelly looked at each other, and then at the danger that awaited them.

CHAPTER

Tom and Randolf had caught up with Percival, Roderick, and the kids, and were fleeing the marketplace. They'd tried to lose their pursuers at every turn, but the Rats and their riders had proved persistent and were close behind them as they burst from the forest into the clearing.

Tom had begun screaming for Lorimar's help as soon as the floating ship became visible through the trees, and now as he raced into the open area, he could just make out a flurry of movement on the ship's deck.

He glanced quickly to his right. Percival was carrying a frying pan, and the twins and Roderick, all wearing pots on their heads, were right with him, running as fast as they could.

Tom then glanced to his left to make sure that Randolf had kept up, but found that he was no longer there. He slowed to look over his shoulder and saw that the Veni Yan had stopped and was standing at the ready with his sword.

"Randolf, what are you doing? Come on!" Tom yelled.

"Get them to the ship," the Veni Yan hollered breathlessly. "I'll buy you some time."

"Tom?" Percival called. He and the others had slowed as well.

"Go!" Tom waved them on. "Get to the ship . . . get Lorimar!" he ordered. "I'm going to help Randolf." He was still gripping the short sword, the dagger stuck through the loop of his tunic belt.

"Give 'em a couple-a good pokes for me," the Bone said, then turned back toward the ship, grabbed the kids, and ran.

Tom joined the Veni Yan priest, strangely not as afraid as he was before.

Maybe he was getting the hang of this hero thing after all.

The Constable rode his mount closer, clutching its thick fur in his hands and watching the two figures ahead: the boy and the priest. He grinned, all teeth with little humor.

He would deal with these two first, then move on to the sky ship. The master would be very pleased by his actions today, and who knew — maybe as a reward, the great and powerful Nacht would let him keep this body of flesh he possessed. The evil spirit had grown quite fond of it.

The Rat Creatures were almost upon their human foes, the two of them standing there pretending to be brave. But the Constable knew they were afraid — how could they not be? They were about to die.

He leaned down close to his beast's ear and hollered, "Stop!"

As usual, the filthy creature did not listen.

"I said stop!" the Constable repeated, drawing his sword and poking the Rat Creature in the head.

The monster stopped, and the others of the ferocious pack followed suit. The Constable could see expressions of surprise on the faces of the boy and Veni Yan as he dismounted, gesturing for his fellow evil spirits to join him. The Rats, seething balls of fur and rage, started to advance as well.

"You will keep back," the Constable ordered the Rats forcefully. "These two belong to us."

The Rats looked as though they had been physically struck.

"The fleshy mammals belong just as much to us as to you. I thought us partners," complained King Agak. "We allow you to ride us, and help you track your enemies." The other Rats nodded in agreement.

The mere suggestion that these vile beings were anything other than tools for the Constable and his men made him want to laugh. But the Rats still had their use, and the Constable had to remember that.

"Partners we are, my furry brother, but this requires a more careful hand," he explained.

"We would be careful," King Agak growled as the other Rats nodded again. "We would be very careful as we rip them apart and gorge ourselves upon their soft, fleshy insides." He had begun to drool.

"Oh, I have no doubt," the Constable said placatingly. "But let's just say that we need to do this ourselves, and leave it at that."

The possessed Constable turned away from the slavering monster, sword in hand, and began to advance toward his still-waiting enemies.

He wanted to be the one to kill them, the one to tell his master in darkness that he had succeeded.

Again, the Constable grinned.

A smile all teeth and no humor.

"What are they doing?" Tom asked Randolf.

"Probably trying to figure out who will get to kill us," Randolf said, watching their adversaries with a careful eye.

"Oh," the boy responded.

"You still have time to leave," Randolf told Tom. "I have enough fight left in me to allow you to get to the ship."

"No," Tom replied stubbornly. "If you're staying, so am I. It's what the leader of a quest should do."

Randolf looked at the boy from the corner of his eye. Perhaps there was more to this Tom Elm than he had given him credit for. Perhaps the Dreaming knew what she was doing, after all.

But now wasn't the time for such thoughts. The four possessed lawmen began to circle them.

"Back to me, boy," Randolf ordered, motioning for Tom to place his back against the priest's own. "That way we can see them from all sides."

The boy did as he was told, and through his robes Randolf could feel the slight tremble of Tom's fear.

"Now what?" Tom asked.

"It's simple, really," the Veni Yan priest said. "Stay low, guard your face and chest, and if any of them come close enough, strike with your sword."

"How hard?" Tom asked.

"As hard as needed to hurt them badly," Randolf said, the words leaving his lips just as the Constable sprang. "Give it all you've got."

The Constable's sword descended in a blurred arc, but Randolf was not in the mood to be sliced down the middle. He brought his own sword up, blocking the weapon and parrying it aside.

The possessed lawman leaped back with murder in his dark eyes.

"Why fight it, priest?" he asked. "It's only a matter of time before your strength falters and you fall before my superior might."

But the Constable's words were suddenly drowned out by another voice in Randolf's mind, the voice of the ancient fortune-teller from the marketplace.

"A dark future for us all unless the mission succeeds," he heard the old woman's voice croak. *"It cannot succeed without your courage."*

Without your courage.

The words filled him with a strength he had not felt in a long time. The Veni Yan priest roared with fury and surged forward, sword at the ready.

Tom watched the grinning deputies, his short sword poised for action.

Their eyes were solid black in the late afternoon sunlight. They, too, studied their opponents, waiting for the right moment to strike.

It was Randolf's sudden cry, followed by a change in the deputies' expressions, that made Tom turn toward the priest.

The Veni Yan had moved away and was attacking the

Constable with a ferocious intensity, wielding the ancient sword with a skill that would have made the captain of Queen Thorn's guard envious.

He rained blow after relentless blow upon the possessed man, driving him back inch by inch, yard by yard, until he was back amongst the Rats. Randolf kept at the Constable, swinging his weapon again and again, finally shattering the villain's sword and knocking him to the ground at the feet of the Rats.

Tom held his breath, but Randolf pulled back, standing over the Constable and breathing heavily.

"Do you yield?" he asked, his voice sounding stronger than Tom remembered hearing before.

The Constable slowly raised his eyes. "Your mercy will be the death of you, and the others," he snarled. "Take them!" he shouted.

And the Rats and deputies swarmed.

Tom and Randolf were drawn together again, back-to-back as the monsters converged upon them.

Tom caught the Veni Yan's eye. "No fear," the priest said, raising his sword.

"No fear," the boy repeated, lifting the short sword in one hand and pulling the dagger from his belt with the other.

Since taking up the mantle of the Dreaming, Tom had

wondered what it would be like to face death, what shape it would come in. And now, as the Rats stalked ever closer, and the Constable's men raised their swords to strike, he knew.

He clutched his weapons tighter and prepared for the worst.

And that was when he felt it, warm against the skin of his chest. The fragment of Spark hanging around his neck was growing hotter. Instinctively he reached beneath his tunic to remove the stone, but as soon as his hand touched it, light exploded from the shard, beaming out from between his fingers and even from his clothes.

The explosion of radiance made the Rat Creatures hiss and the possessed lawmen scream, all of them trying to hide their faces from the light.

Tom remained frozen in place, visions of the Dreaming filling his mind. He saw a dark and mysterious cave, this time clearer and more distinct . . . rife with tunnels and three looming beasts, and bees . . . so many bees . . . their bodies so large that they blotted out the sun, their humming voices drowning out all sound.

And then everything turned to gold — gold so intense that he felt he was drowning in it, but he wasn't afraid.

As the visions faded, Tom realized that he was no longer standing and facing death, but moving.

Bouncing up and down, as a matter of fact.

He gave his head a good shake to clear away the confusion and realized he was hanging over Randolf's shoulder, the Veni Yan priest carrying him as he ran across the clearing toward the *Queen of the Sky*. In the distance, he could see that the monsters had recovered and were again in pursuit.

"Put me down!" Tom screamed, kicking his feet. "I can run!"

Randolf barely slowed down while he leaned slightly to the left, allowing Tom's feet to touch the ground.

"Are you sure you're all right?" the priest asked as Tom stumbled, then caught his balance, and ran to catch up.

"I'm fine," he answered. "Sorry, I don't know what happened back there."

"There'll be time for explanations later," Randolf said, glancing over his shoulder, "if we survive."

The monsters were gaining, and Tom doubted either of them had the strength to fight back. He felt as though he was running in a nightmare, the sky ship never any closer. Soon Randolf began to slow down.

"Don't think about it," Tom told him, reaching out to grab his arm, trying to lend him what little energy he had left. "We're going to do this . . . we're going to reach the ship . . . we're almost there. . . ."

And then he saw it, up ahead and moving closer, two more large, furry shapes coming at them with great speed.

For a moment he thought the evil Rats had somehow flanked them, but then he caught sight of the riders and knew that help had finally arrived.

Percival was astride Smelly, holding on for dear life; Roderick and the twins rode Stinky.

And the two Rats looked terrified.

Percival held tightly to Smelly's surprisingly soft, pointed ears, using the fleshy protrusions to steer the shaggy beast. It reminded him of some of the steering mechanisms on board the *Queen of the Sky* — only the *Queen* didn't scream when he steered her.

A quick glance to the right showed him that the kids were doing all right atop Stinky. Barclay and Abbey each held an ear, while Roderick — perched in the middle — navigated.

Tom and Randolf were just up ahead, but things didn't look good. The Rats and the deputies were right behind them, and by the way the two were stumbling around, it didn't look as though they had much juice left.

"Faster!" Percival urged, yanking on Smelly's ears.

"YEEEEOWWWW!" Smelly wailed, as he pumped his four muscular limbs even harder. "Those are still attached!"

Not to be outdone, Abbey and Barclay got their Rat moving faster as well.

"AAAARRRRRGGGGHHHHH!" Stinky screamed, running as if trying to escape the little creatures perched on his back. "This is for Fredrick . . . this is for Fredrick . . . this is for Fredrick . . ." the Rat Creature repeated, over and over.

Percival could see it was going to be tight. They probably had just enough time to snatch up the boy and the old man and turn around, but it was going to be close.

"C'mon, give me everything you've got," Percival said, bending low and pulling on Smelly's ears.

"I'm giving! I'm giving!" the Rat yelled.

They were almost there.

Almost.

There.

Tom and Randolf were suddenly before them.

"Whoa!" Percival yelled, yanking back to bring the powerful beast to a grass-flying stop.

"Quick, climb on!" the Bone ordered, and Tom did as he was told.

Percival kicked his heels into Smelly's sides, bringing him back around Stinky, who had slowed to let Randolf climb on. They were about to begin their furious run back to the sky ship, when Roderick lost his grip and tumbled from Stinky's back.

"Wait!" Percival commanded, again pulling the creature's head back.

Tom was already on the move, sliding from Smelly's back to rescue his friend, but it was too late. The bad guys were running so fast, there was no chance of stopping, and poor little Roderick was directly in their path. Tom snatched the raccoon up in his arms, and turned his back to the advancing horde.

Percival didn't want to watch, but he couldn't look away.

Tom took Roderick into his arms and shielded the little raccoon's body with his own, preparing to be trampled.

He braced himself, a million things running through his mind as he crouched there, waiting for the inevitable. What would happen to his family? What about the quest? Would the others keep going? Would the Dreaming speak to them as well?

Would the Nacht be victorious?

The ground shook beneath his knees and he screamed, waiting for the pain.

But it didn't come.

He opened his eyes. A barrier of thick, twisting, thorn-covered vines had suddenly grown across the entire length of the clearing, separating Tom and Roderick from the fearsome horde.

"Wow, will you look at that," Roderick said, reaching out a tentative paw toward the wall of vines. A Rat Creature's claw shot through an opening in the thicket, and Tom yanked Roderick back from its reach.

"Careful," he said as he and his pal backed away from the barrier.

"I bet I know where that came from," Roderick said as they listened to the monsters growl and howl in fury on the other side.

"I think I have an idea, too," Tom answered. He didn't want to be unappreciative, but he wondered what had taken Lorimar so long to help them.

"C'mon, Tom, before they figure out how to get over," Percival called out from his Rat Creature mount.

Tom didn't need to be told twice. He and Roderick turned and hopped up onto Stinky's back, and then all of them returned to the waiting *Queen of the Sky* to finally make good their escape.

"No!" King Agak screeched, grabbing hold of the vines before him and giving them a violent shake as he watched his enemies get away.

He whipped around, fixing his Rat soldiers in his freezing stare.

"What are you standing around for?" he growled. "Climb over the wall! Get me those who would dare steal from their king. . . . Get me my squirrel!"

The Rats cautiously approached the wall and tried to scale it, but the thorns were too many and too sharp, and they didn't meet with much success.

This infuriated the King all the more, and he turned his wrath on the humans that weren't quite human.

"You!" he roared, pointing a gnarled, clawed finger at the leader of their allies. "You promised the usurpers would be mine . . . that the squirrel would be returned." He got down on all fours and padded menacingly closer to the Constable. "And you promised me Bones," he continued. "I have never tasted Bones," he added, shaking his shaggy head.

Saliva dribbled uncontrollably from the Rat King's mouth, and he realized that he had not eaten lately. Suddenly, the aroma of the not-so-human humans was strangely enticing.

Agak moved closer, but the Constable held his ground. "I'm disappointed, too," he said.

The King watched as the Constable stepped toward the obstruction that had robbed them of their prize and pressed his face to an opening in the vines.

"But we won't let a little disappointment spoil our special friendship, will we?" The Constable turned to look at Agak, his dark eyes fixed to the Rat's.

And suddenly the King had no interest in sampling the

meat of these inhuman humans, certain that if he did, he'd suffer a severe bout of stomach discomfort for sure.

"No," King Agak replied, his Rat soldiers milling around him.

"Good," the Constable said with a disarming smile. Then he motioned toward his deputies.

"Cut an opening," he ordered as they drew their swords. "And make it snappy."

CHAPTER 7

Tom looked up at Stinky's hairy behind and, for a moment, wondered why he had insisted on being last up the rope ladder to the *Queen of the Sky*.

He turned his head to look at the wall of thorny vines in the distance. He could see movement as pieces of the dark green growth fell away.

"Would you hurry up, please?" Tom asked, reaching up to give the large, furry buttocks above him a poke.

"EEEEKKK!" the Rat yelled. "I'm being attacked from behind!"

"It's me," Tom called up to him, annoyed. "Speed it up. The Constable and his men are breaking through the vines."

The Rat twisted on the rope ladder, fixing Tom in an icy stare. "I'm going as fast as I can, mammal, and jabbing me in the posterior isn't going to help me move any faster, thank you very much."

The Constable and his men tore through the vines, the eager Rats right behind them.

"How about your Rat King getting here any minute and taking away Fredrick," Tom suggested. "Will that make you move faster?"

"I'm climbing! I'm climbing!" Stinky said, picking up the pace.

Tom watched the large, furry behind disappear over the side of the sky craft, and immediately followed.

"Time to go," he ordered as his feet touched the deck.

"Sounds like a plan." Percival was already running toward the wheelhouse.

Abbey, with Roderick's help, started to haul in the ladder, while Barclay went to work pulling up the anchor.

The Rats had retreated to their corner of the craft, Stinky cradling his dead squirrel while Smelly placed a comforting arm around his friend, whispering reassurances.

Randolf crouched nearby, tending to some deep scratches on his arm, and Tom headed toward him.

"It's best to wash these right away," Randolf said, using a ragged piece of cloth and some water to cleanse the angry-looking wounds. "Wouldn't want to lose the arm to infection."

"No, that wouldn't be good at all," the boy agreed. "We're going to need both your arms if we're going to succeed on this quest."

Randolf gave Tom a cautious look from the corner of his eye. "The quest," he said, tending his wounds. "If today was any example of what is to come, we're likely to need a lot more than just my two arms to survive."

The Veni Yan's eyes moved across the deck, observing the motley crew in action as the sky craft made its escape.

"You work with what you have," Tom said.

"What?" the priest asked.

"It's something my father always said." The image of his parents and little sister filled Tom's head. "You work with what you have. I know we don't look like much," he continued, "but the Dreaming picked us."

"I seriously question the sanity of the Dreaming," Randolf said as he finished dressing his wounds. "Although you handled yourself well out there today."

The corners of Tom's mouth started to turn up with pride.

"For a boy," the Veni Yan added, and Tom's smile quickly faded.

"We're going to need much more than a boy if we're going to find the remaining pieces of the Spark and prevent the Nacht from overtaking the Valley," Randolf warned.

Tom knew the priest was right. He'd struggled with the same idea since he'd begun this quest. What did he know about being a leader? He was just a boy . . . a turnip farmer.

"You're right," he said, removing the fragment of Spark that hung around his neck. "What do I know about leading quests? You should be wearing this." He held the fragment out toward Randolf.

"Oh no," the priest said with a shake of his head. "You were chosen, not I."

"But you said —"

"I said that this quest is going to need more than a boy to lead it." Randolf picked up the bowl of water he had been using to clean his wounds, and pitched it over the side of the ship. "Let us see if the Dreaming chose wisely."

And with those words, the priest walked away, leaving Tom alone with his doubts and the crushing weight of the responsibility that remained his.

As he slowly placed the Spark back around his neck, he sensed that he was no longer alone. He turned to find Lorimar standing behind him.

"Is everything all right, Lorimar?" Tom asked.

"I must speak with you," she said in a dire tone, and Tom immediately thought she had bad news from the Dreaming. Maybe she was going to tell him that he wasn't doing a good enough job and was no longer responsible.

For a moment, he half hoped that was so.

"I'm sorry I failed you and the others," Lorimar said sadly.

"Failed us?" Tom questioned. "How did you do that?"

"When you were calling for my aid."

"You helped us by growing that wall of vines," Tom said.

"If it weren't for the two Rats, you would have fallen to the Nacht's servants," she said, with a rustling shake of her leafy head.

"But we didn't." Tom reached out and touched the rough skin of her arm. "There's no need to worry."

She fixed him in a freezing stare.

"You are wrong, Tom Elm," Lorimar said. "I do worry. Something prevents me from being entirely here for you, and for the quest."

"What is it?" Tom asked.

"Voices," Lorimar whispered, turning her gaze beyond the flying ship.

"Voices?"

"The voices of my people . . . the First Folk . . ."

Lorimar looked intently at Tom, and he saw on her face a look that he'd never seen before, one of excitement.

"They are alive, and they are calling to me."

"But you said you were the last," Tom said.

"And that is what I have believed these many years, but now they call out to me, begging for my help."

"Where are they?" Tom asked. "Maybe we can all go and —"

"No," Lorimar said. "Where I need to go, you of flesh and blood will be unable to travel."

The sudden realization hit him like a rock to the forehead.

"You're leaving us . . . you're leaving the quest."

"For now," Lorimar confirmed. "But I will rejoin you as soon as I am able."

She reached up to the branches that made up her hair and pulled on a section of leaves. "Here," she said, holding out a cluster of acorns. "Take these with you so that I may follow when I am able."

"Are you sure?" Tom asked. "Are you sure we can't help?"

The tree woman shook her leafy head.

"Even now they call to me. Their cries are bringing me to the brink of insanity. If I am ever to be of use on this quest, I must go."

"All right." Tom nodded. "When will you be leaving?"

"I can wait no longer," Lorimar said. "I go in search of them now."

And before he could even say good-bye, the plant woman's body broke apart and fell to the deck — devoid of Lorimar's animating spirit.

The Constable watched as the sky ship drifted away over the treetops. *We were so close*, he thought, burning with frustration.

"We should go after them," King Agak said from beside him.

"No," the Constable replied. He was tired of the running and the failure. "Their ship will outdistance us in a matter of minutes."

This was the second time their quarry had escaped with the help of their flying craft. If it weren't for that sky ship . . .

And then the Constable had an idea.

The sky ship was the key. Take it away and the Dreaming's champions would never be able to escape them.

"Why are you snarling?" Agak asked, watching the Constable with curious, black eyes.

"I'm not snarling, I'm smiling," the evil spirit said.

"What do you have to smile about? We've lost them — again."

The Constable ignored the Rat King and gestured for his fellow spirits to come closer.

"I have an idea," he said to his brethren.

"Tell us," demanded one of the deputies.

"Twice the enemies of our Lord and Master have escaped in the air," the Constable said, pretending that his hand was the sky craft and sailing it past the deputies' faces.

"Yes," agreed one.

"That's right," said another. "It's not fair they have a ship that sails the sky."

"Not fair at all," the third admitted, angrily folding his arms across his chest.

"Exactly," said the Constable. "But what if we were able to . . ." He brought his hand down and hid it behind his back. "Take it away."

His deputies smiled.

"Then there would be no way for them to escape us," a deputy said, and the others nodded in agreement.

"Exactly."

King Agak and his Rat followers had moved closer to listen.

"You plan to take their sky ship from them?" the Rat leader asked with a tilt of his shaggy head.

"That's what I'm thinking," the Constable replied.

King Agak laughed, and his soldiers did the same. "And how do you intend to do that?" he asked. "Are you going to reach up and pluck it from the sky? Or perhaps you will sprout wings, like a bird, and drive it down to the ground?"

The Rats were all laughing riotously, amused by their King's sarcasm. Their insolence bothered the deputies.

"Silence!" one of them bellowed.

"Cease your irksome noise, Rats!" said another.

"Our leader will tell us how he plans to bring his plan to fruition," added the third. "You are planning on telling us, aren't you?" he asked the Constable from a corner of his mouth.

"I am," the Constable confirmed. He waited until all their eager eyes were on him.

"Well?" King Agak prodded.

The Constable turned his eyes to the heavens. Clouds were building — a storm was on its way.

"We shall ride the winds and drive the craft from the air."

"Ride the winds?" Agak repeated. "How, by Great Queen Maude's tail, do you plan on doing that?"

The Constable glared at the Rat King and his followers. "You forget, Hairy Men, that we are not what we appear to be," he said. "The flesh you see is but a cloak we wear, easily discarded to reveal our true nature."

King Agak cocked his head inquisitively to one side. "True nature?"

"Spirits," the Constable hissed. "Evil spirits."

A spark of realization appeared in the Rat King's round, glistening eyes.

"Evil spirits," he repeated.

"What do you mean she's gone?" Abbey asked, concern in her young voice.

"Is she coming back?" Roderick wanted to know.

"What are we going to do?" Barclay questioned. "She had all kinds of special powers and stuff. How are we going to complete the quest without her?"

"We'll be fine." Tom tried to reassure them, even though he wasn't feeling that great about Lorimar's decision to leave either. "She isn't gone forever. There were just some things she had to check into about her people."

Percival was leaning against the doorway to the wheelhouse, the *Queen of the Sky* now flying on automatic. "I thought she said she was the last of the First Folk."

"She did," Tom said. "But now she says she can hear them calling her, asking for help. What could she do?"

"Lorimar did what she had to do," Randolf answered. "But it does not change the fact that she and her unique abilities will be severely missed."

"She had powers," Barclay whined. "None of us have any powers. We're doomed!"

"Hey, stop that kind of talk," Percival warned his nephew.

"Yeah, knock it off, brainless," Abbey echoed. "We'll be perfectly fine without her. . . . Right, Tom?"

"Right, Abbey," Tom said, concentrating on not showing how worried he really was. "We might not have powers, but we're all pretty special."

Barclay remained silent, evidently not convinced of their specialness.

"Well, look at Randolf here. He's a great warrior," Tom said, pointing out the old priest, who seemed embarrassed by the attention. "And your uncle Percival is a great explorer, inventor, and pilot of a really cool sky ship."

Tom looked at the other members of the quest.

"Abbey is very smart, and a big help at reminding us to keep the *Queen of the Sky* tidy."

The little Bone crossed her arms and smiled proudly. "A clean sky ship is a happy sky ship," she said.

Tom went on. "Roderick knows a lot about the Valley and is very small and sneaky."

"Sneaky in a good way," the raccoon added.

"And the Dreaming communicates with me through my Spark necklace. . . ."

"And I know how to pilot the *Queen of the Sky* and I'm pretty strong," Barclay said, flexing his arm to show off a tiny muscle.

"Exactly," Tom said enthusiastically.

"What about them?" Abbey asked, pointing to the two Rat Creatures sitting side by side.

Tom found himself at a loss for words.

"Ah, they . . ."

Everybody was waiting.

"I've been told I have a lovely singing voice," Stinky offered.

"That's very true," Smelly agreed. "And I can make a fabulous quiche."

The crew of the *Queen* just stared at the two hairy beasts, nobody sure how to respond.

"What's a quiche?" Barclay asked, breaking the silence.

"It doesn't matter," Tom interjected before the Rat could answer. "You see, we all have our special talents. We'll do just fine until Lorimar gets back."

"I guess you're right," Barclay said. "We wouldn't have

been chosen by the Dreaming if we couldn't do the job."

"That's right," Tom agreed, even though he still had his doubts. He looked to Randolf, who quickly averted his eyes. "The Dreaming thinks we can do it, and we will."

"So what's next?" Abbey asked.

Tom was about to answer, when Percival cleared his throat.

"Yes, Percival?" Tom asked.

"Since our last little expedition didn't go quite as planned, we're going to need supplies pretty quickly." The Bone looked out at the propellers. "If we don't get our hands on some potatoes soon, we're not going to have the power to keep us moving."

"We have to find some potatoes, then," Tom said, feeling what optimism he had mustered begin to wane.

"In my early days, I ran across some farms not too far from here," Randolf volunteered. He looked out at the countryside passing below them. "Perhaps they would take pity on us and spare some potatoes."

"It's worth a try," Tom said. "What do you think, Percival?"

The explorer was looking warily at the sky. Tom did the same, and saw that thick, gray clouds had started to gather. From somewhere in the distance, he could hear a faint rumble of thunder.

"I think we might need to set down for a bit," Percival said. "My nose tells me this storm could be nasty." He pointed to his face. "And the nose always knows."

Tom continued to stare up into the sky at the clouds that now roiled and churned above them. Curious how a storm could spring up so suddenly when it had been such a perfect day. It seemed . . . *unnatural*.

CHAPTER 8

In all his years, King Agak had never seen anything so strange. Where the sky above him had once been blue and cloudless, it now raged with a ferocious storm.

And it was the humans' doing — the humans who did not really smell like humans at all.

The one who called himself the Constable gathered his minions in the clearing where they had lost their prey. The thought of his dead squirrel and three delicious Bones floating away still filled him with unbridled fury, but he did his best to contain himself. Such rage wasn't good for his gizzard; at least that's what old Doc Guam had told him.

The Constable ordered the Rat Creatures to form a circle around him and his deputies. Agak considered arguing, but ultimately decided to give the Constable one last chance.

"Why are we doing this?" the King asked as he motioned his soldiers to join him.

"Because once our spirits leave these bodies, their original inhabitants will return and will probably try to run away. And we like these bodies."

"So you wish us to keep them from escaping?" Agak asked.

"Precisely." The Constable joined hands with the three deputies. "We'll be back shortly."

"My patience grows thin," Agak snarled at the mammal leader.

"And it will be rewarded," the Constable assured him. "As soon as we leave these bodies, we will commune with the elements of the sky, and bring that ship crashing to earth."

"And into our clutches," the Rat King added.

"Exactly," the Constable agreed.

"See that you don't disappoint us again," Agak warned, and his soldiers hissed and growled. "We would hate to have to snack upon the human bodies that you've grown so fond of."

The Constable's black eyes flashed with anger, but the rage did not go any further.

Perhaps the Constable has concerns about his gizzard as well, the King of the Rat Creatures considered.

Instead, the Constable turned his attention to his deputies. "Shall we proceed?"

They all nodded and, still holding hands, closed their eyes. Their bodies grew limp, and they dropped to the ground as if suddenly bereft of bones.

The Rat Creatures were sorely tempted to snack on the bodies — which were now smelling as scrumptious as a human body should — but then Agak caught sight of the ghostly shapes drifting upward.

They were what had taken up residence inside the humans, making their stink so different. The King and his soldiers watched with fascination while the wispy creatures, looking as if they were made from thick swaths of spiderweb, darted about for a moment, and then — in a flash — up into the sky. It wasn't long before it started to darken as thick, gray clouds began to form. The thunder growled like Agak's empty stomach.

Impressive, the Rat King thought as the storm raged above him. *Perhaps these spirit creatures will actually be able to accomplish what they've promised.*

For their sake, King Agak hoped that to be true.

For the humans within the circle had begun to stir, and were looking quite tasty indeed.

Percival firmly gripped the *Queen*'s wheel with both hands, fighting the power of the storm as it tried to wrestle control away from him.

The storm had materialized out of nowhere. His sensitive nose had noticed a hint of storminess, but he never imagined the winds would be whacking his ship around like a child playing too roughly with a new toy.

The wheel shook violently, and through the window of the wheelhouse, he saw only gray, churning clouds, punctuated by flashes of lightning and deafening thunderclaps. The gauges before him showed that the *Queen of the Sky* was performing as best she could in the furious winds, but it wasn't good enough if they wanted to escape the storm. They needed more power.

"Is there anything I should do?" Tom yelled over the howling wind, holding on to the door frame to keep from stumbling.

"Well, if you don't have any potatoes on you, I think it might be wise to get everybody below deck," Percival said as he gripped the wheel. It felt like he was having a wrestling match with the meanest kid on the block, who just happened to be three hundred feet tall and as strong as forty oxen. "I think this ride is about to get worse."

"This isn't a normal storm," Tom shouted from the doorway.

Percival was about to respond, when he saw them: strange, ghostly shapes dancing in the wind.

"No," he agreed quietly, "this isn't a normal storm."

The winds shrieked louder and the *Queen of the Sky* shook even more, as if the ship itself were afraid.

. . .

The evil spirits soared, tormenting the clouds and relent-
lessly assaulting the elements. It was they who brought the
storm, who coaxed the pelting rain and shrieking winds,
the searing lightning and roaring thunder.

The spirit leader surged toward the sky craft, catching
a quick glimpse of the boy leader and the others who had
taken up arms against his master. The ship heaved and
dipped in the grip of the storm, the Bone captain trying
desperately to ride out the squall.

It would be for naught. This storm was too wild — too
powerful to be ridden.

But as much as he took joy from the spirits' wicked actions, the leader missed the Constable's body, which he had
left in the care of his Rat allies, and he was sure that his
brothers felt the same. He loved the fleshy body he'd been
wearing, experiencing the world in ways he never could've
imagined — the smells, the sounds, the sensations.

The spirits became even more aggressive, and the storm
responded in kind, growing larger and even more violent.
The sky ship was like a leaf caught in the hold of a hur-
ricane. As he watched the winds assail the wooden craft,
the leader was certain his master would be proud of him.

He hoped that he and his brothers would be rewarded
for their efforts.

• • •

Tom clung to the railing of the *Queen of the Sky* as he carefully moved across the deck toward the others, who were huddled beneath a tarp at the bow of the ship. He glanced up at the sky, catching a glimpse of three spectral shapes that were circling the three balloons holding the *Queen* aloft.

The ship suddenly dipped beneath his feet and he lost his grip on the rail. He fell on his butt and started to slide down the deck toward the front of the craft, desperately searching for something — *anything* — to grab on to.

The wind pushed the ship back up, and Tom was temporarily halted, but then he tumbled back the other way, along with everything on the deck that wasn't tied down. Percival shouted his name as he slid past the wheelhouse, but the boy couldn't stop.

Ahead of him, an empty wooden crate hit the stern and flipped over the side of the ship, and Tom scrabbled for anything that would stop him from following it into oblivion. Above the moan of the winds and the crashes of thunder, he could just barely hear what sounded like maniacal laughter.

Tom strained his fingers, scraping his nails across the solid wood of the deck as the side of the *Queen* loomed closer. He braced himself, hoping he could grab hold of the rail as he was about to go over.

Just then, something snagged his collar, bringing him

to an abrupt and violent standstill. He lay on the deck for a moment, afraid to move. Then he took a deep breath and turned to see what had stopped his fall — and gazed into the round, bulbous eyes of a Rat Creature.

Smelly had hooked Tom's collar on one of his long claws.

"Thank you," Tom offered, as the deck continued to pitch and yaw.

"Don't thank me, mammal," the Rat Creature said. "They made me do it."

Tom lifted his head and looked beyond Smelly to see that a kind of chain had been formed: Randolf was gripping the Rat's other hand, and his robes were being held by the combined might of Abbey, Barclay, and Roderick. They were being held by Stinky, whose other paw grasped the portside rail to support the living chain.

"Well, thanks anyway," Tom said, just as a flash of lightning illuminated the sky, and thunder exploded. "We need to get below deck," he hollered as he shakily climbed to his feet.

Randolf grabbed the twins and Roderick and quickly moved them toward the wheelhouse. But the Rats held back, cowering, as the storm seemed to intensify even more.

Tom pushed the beasts toward safety, but just as he was about to enter the wheelhouse behind them, a jag of white-hot energy plunged down from the heavens to strike the deck directly in front of him, tossing him backward like one of his sister's rag dolls.

Tom wasn't sure where he landed, but he landed hard. The world grew fuzzy, the sounds of the storm growing softer as he slipped from consciousness into the dark and silent place beneath it.

The humans were awake, but the Rat Creatures were ready.

"Where . . . where are we?" the true Constable asked. He pretended to be brave, but Agak knew better. The King could smell his fear.

The humans were standing in a circle, back-to-back. They had immediately drawn their weapons and were holding them in trembling hands. The Rat King hoped they wouldn't be stupid enough to use them, for he doubted that he and his soldiers would be able to restrain themselves.

"How did we get here?" the Constable asked. He raised a dagger. "Tell me or . . . or I'll gouge out your eyes."

Agak laughed at his bravado. "Do you not remember, mammal?" the Rat King teased. "You rode our backs."

The smell of fear became even stronger.

"You . . . you lie!" said one of the three deputies, shaking a short sword. The King's soldiers laughed at that.

"Why would we lie?" the Rat King asked, tilting his head playfully to one side. "What would we gain by that?"

The men looked at each other fearfully.

"The last thing I remember was being at the jail . . . and falling asleep," the Constable said to his deputies in a quavering voice. "And . . . and I had the most horrible dream. . . ."

"Yes," agreed another of the deputies. "I remember a dream, too . . . a terrible dream. . . ."

"A nightmare," offered the third deputy. "It was awful. . . ."

The Constable turned his frightened gaze to the Rat King. "I dreamed that something crossed over from the darkness," he said, his voice a shaky whisper. "Crossed over and took control of . . . of my body."

The smell of fear wafting off of the humans was intoxicating, and Agak's empty stomach began to rumble and grumble, much like the storm that still reverberated above their heads. His soldiers looked at him, and he could tell by the look in their eyes that they were hungry, too.

How pathetic the humans looked, standing there clumped together, their posturing gradually falling away.

Pathetic and oh so tasty, thought Agak. "Maybe it would be acceptable if we only ate one of them," he suggested aloud, looking to his soldiers.

They vigorously nodded their heads, thick, pink tongues snaking out to lick at leathery lips.

The Rats began to advance upon the huddled humans,

when Agak sensed something in the air. The thick hair at the nape of his neck was suddenly alert, standing on end as an odd sensation vibrated through his monstrous body.

The King looked above him. The rain had slowed, and he could make out three wraithlike shapes as they descended from the sky.

"Curses," he snarled, realizing that the evil spirits had returned for their human bodies.

His soldiers harrumphed their disappointment, sucking their long tongues back into their mouths as they all watched the spirits land upon the humans like a net of spider's silk. The humans cried out and trembled violently, but soon they closed their eyes and there was only silence.

King Agak waited, watching the humans stand very still, their heads bowed as if asleep. He padded closer to sniff at the bodies — they smelled different now. Inhuman.

The Constable's eyes snapped open, revealing glistening orbs of solid darkness. Instinctively, King Agak drew back with a hiss.

"It's done," the Constable said. "The sky ship flies no more."

CHAPTER 9

The last thing Tom remembered thinking about before being tossed through the air was his sister. Or more specifically, one of her rag dolls.

He'd always hated her dolls — their simple faces and button eyes made him feel uneasy for some reason. And he was staring into a pair of those very button eyes when he opened his own.

"Are you awake, Tommy?" asked his sister in the strange squeaky voice that she gave to her dolls.

"Lottie?" he asked, struggling to sit up and getting a face full of rag doll. "Is that you?"

"Who else would it be?" She giggled and pulled her doll away, hugging it close.

Tom quickly looked around. The landscape was dark and rocky, the sky above a cold gray. "Where am I?" he asked, trying to shrug off the dullness of sleep.

"No time for that," Lottie said importantly, turning around and scrambling up a rocky slope behind her. "We have to go."

"Go where?" Tom asked as he climbed to his feet and followed the little girl.

She didn't answer him, but as they reached a small plateau, he saw that his parents were there as well.

"Come along, Tom," his father called, motioning for him to follow.

"Come along, Tom," Lottie repeated, using her squeaky doll voice.

"You heard your father, boy," Tom's mother said sternly. "We need to find cover." She took Lottie's hand, pulling her along, following his father.

"Mom . . . Dad," Tom called out as he, too, followed. "How did you get here? Where are we?" He paused to study the cold, harsh environment, and then he heard it on the wind: a soft musical sound calling to him.

"Tom!" his father bellowed.

Startled, the boy looked to where his family waited in the entrance to a cave. Tom didn't remember the large, rocky opening being there just moments ago.

"In here," his father said, motioning for him to follow.

The music came again, drifting on the air, and Tom was pulled toward it. It was strangely soothing — strangely familiar.

He was about to ask his father about it, but his family was gone. He began to panic, moving closer to the cave, calling out to them.

"Mother!"

The ground grew rockier the closer he got.

"Father . . . Lottie?"

"Inside." An unfamiliar voice drifted out from the darkness inside the cave. "Join us. Come inside."

Tom peered into darkness as thick as tar, craning his neck and squinting his eyes, searching for any sign of his family.

"Come. Inside," the voice commanded more forcefully.

He lost his footing on a rounded rock and stumbled, falling beneath a living shadow that surged like a serpent from inside the cave, its cavernous maw snapping at the empty space where he had just been standing. Tom crouched, staring up at the beast with a mixture of wonder and terror. He knew what this was, this monstrous thing.

It was a Dragon . . . a Dragon made of darkness.

"Didn't you hear me, boy?" it asked in a voice that sent tickling vibrations through the air.

There was no doubt that this was the Nacht, and it was horrible. Its eyes were like the embers at the far back of a dwindling stove fire — still very much alive, still burning with life.

"You're a smart one, aren't you, Tom Elm?" the Nacht said in its terrible voice.

Tom didn't move.

"Not fooled by my little tricks to tug at your heart." And with those words the great Dragon of darkness opened wide its mouth and belched a thick, billowing cloud of shadow that took the shape of his little sister.

"Lottie," Tom whispered as the shape broke apart, dispersing like smoke in the wind.

"Very smart," the Nacht growled. "It's probably why she picked you."

Tom noticed the way the beast said the word *she*, as if it were a bitter poison in its mouth. He knew who the great monster was referring to, and took strength from the knowledge that it . . . that *she*, still held some form of power over such a horrible thing.

"She'll beat you," Tom said, trying to stand tall beneath the beast's baleful glare. "*We'll* beat you."

The Dragon leaned in closer to Tom, an awful growl rumbling in the depths of its massive throat, but the boy stood his ground.

Then the Nacht tossed back its head and began to laugh. It was a bone-chilling sound, absent of any mirth, and it sent an icy cold shiver through Tom's body.

"You actually believe you can stop me?" the Nacht asked. "When I am finally able to leave this place . . ."

The words were like a bonk to the head with a stick.

"When I am able to leave this place," Tom repeated to himself, finding power in the words.

"You mock me, boy?" the Nacht asked, nostrils flaring.

Tom stood taller. "You said when you are *able* to leave this place. None of this is real . . . is it?" he asked.

The Dragon roared, snapping at Tom, but the boy held his ground and the Nacht did not touch him.

Could not touch him.

"This is a dream," he told the Dragon. "And you can't hurt me here."

The soft, musical sound that had attracted his interest earlier again danced upon the air, and Tom took strength from its beauty. The Nacht noticed the sound, too.

"That might be true for the moment," the Dragon said.

Tom felt the Spark around his neck begin to grow warm, the light from it escaping through the fabric of his shirt.

The Nacht recoiled with a snarl of his liquid-black lip as Tom withdrew the Spark from his shirt and held it up to the Dragon.

"This will stop you," he said defiantly. "The Spark will stop what you have begun."

The music of the Dreaming was louder now. Tom advanced toward the Nacht, glowing Spark still in hand, and the Dragon slowly backed deeper inside the cave.

"I grow stronger with each passing second," the Nacht growled.

Its huge form of solid black blended with the shadows of the cave. "And soon I will have enough power . . ."

The Nacht fell silent, its foreboding shape invisible in the darkness of the cave, and Tom thought he had won.

"To strike!" the Nacht suddenly roared, swiping at Tom with a clawed limb.

Instinctively, Tom leaped away from the Dragon's attack. He then felt the oddest sensation — as if a piece of ice had been laid upon his chest. He looked down to see a shallow gash had been scratched into his flesh.

But if this isn't real . . . how?

And then it became disturbingly clear, as he felt his body start to slip away, the Waking World calling him back.

The threat was growing stronger.

Tom awoke suddenly, wrapped in darkness. His eyes were open, and he knew that he was no longer dreaming, but he could see nothing. He put his hands out and realized that it wasn't darkness at all, but a heavy, silky fabric.

"Hello?" he called out, kicking against the fabric. "Is anybody there . . . can anybody hear me?"

He was answered by a low, creaking sound. And then the surface upon which he was lying started to slowly rock, up and down.

Tom thrashed all the more, managing to turn onto his stomach under the silky cover. Carefully, he crawled across what felt like the floor of the *Queen*.

"Percival!" he called out. "Randolf? Roderick? Is anybody —"

But before he could finish, he heard a tremendous groan, and the surface beneath him tipped forward, sending him sliding across the floor. He reached out to grab at handfuls of the fabric, but it slipped through his fingers, and suddenly he dropped out from beneath the covering in a flash of brilliance.

A rush of green surged into his face; his hands ripped at leaves, and thick branches knocked the wind from his body. Tom landed hard on a thick tree limb and held on for dear life, breathing deeply as he hugged the branch with both arms and legs. It bobbed with his weight, but didn't break.

He took a moment to pull his fevered thoughts together, then looked up. What he saw made him gasp.

The *Queen of the Sky* sat atop the thick limbs of the gigantic trees around him, her three mighty balloons deflated and draped across the deck — the source of his silky covering.

"Hello?" he called out again, holding tight to the branch. "Is anybody there? . . . Hello?" The *Queen* appeared empty of life, so he turned his attention to getting to the ground below.

The moaning of the trees holding the *Queen of the Sky* aloft made him glance nervously upward as he made his way down. The ship moved ominously from side to side, so he quickened his pace as much as he could.

He stopped for a moment on another thick branch to take stock of his surroundings. These were some of the biggest trees he had ever seen, and he suspected the storm must have blown them farther south into the Valley. Below him, supplies from the *Queen* were strewn about the ground, but still there was no sign of his friends.

"Percival!" he called out again. "Where are you?"

He finally reached the ground, dropping carefully onto the forest floor. The woods were thick, green, and wet from the powerful storm. Still his friends were nowhere to be found.

What if they'd been blown overboard by the storm, and he was the only one left? His heart hammered in his chest, and he quickly pushed the horrible thought to the back of his mind.

He reached up and touched the Spark, which made him feel better, safer. He remembered his dream and looked down to see the angry scratch on his chest left by the Nacht's attack. His sweat made it sting.

A rustle of leaves nearby distracted him from his dreamtime injury, and he spun around toward the sound.

"Hello?" he called out. "Is anybody there?"

A low humming filled the air around him and he froze. Tom had heard that sound before — in the most recent visions given to him by the Spark. It was the sound of giant bees.

Cautiously, Tom pulled aside some thick pine branches and headed toward the source of the humming — and ran smack into a wall.

Except that walls weren't usually covered with fur.

Tom looked up into the face of one of the largest bears he had ever seen. A quick look to the left, and then the right, showed that there were other bears of varying heights, one on either side of the largest.

The bears were standing upright, glaring at him — and at their feet lay his unconscious friends.

He was about to call out to them, but the large bear standing in front of him pulled back a massive paw and swatted Tom across the top of the head. Tom's world exploded into stars as the sound of giant bees buzzed louder.

The journey through the woods, hanging from a bear's mouth, wasn't a gentle one, and another nasty bump on the head wasn't what Percival needed. Having barely survived the *Queen*'s crash landing during the storm, the Bone adventurer hadn't even had a chance to catch his breath before he, Randolf, and the kids were attacked by the three hairy brutes as they wandered the forest, looking for Tom.

And then there were Stinky and Smelly. Percival had no idea what had happened to those two, but from the corner of his eye, he saw that Tom had joined their troupe, his unconscious body slung over the back of the largest of the bears, along with Randolf. He was about to say something to the boy, when suddenly, things went dark and cool. They'd entered a cave.

"Put 'em in a pile," he heard one of the bears gruffly command. "And then we'll figure out what to do with them."

Percival's blood went cold. If they didn't do something quick, they were as good as eaten for sure. The Bone explorer's mind raced. He remembered a similar incident, when he'd been captured by the Tons'a Fon tribe on the unexplored island of Beafjurky in the southernmost region of the Salty Seas. Surrounded by spear-toting warriors, he'd discovered that the tribe harbored a communal sweet tooth, and had managed to gain their trust with a package of chocolate-covered dingleberries that he'd saved from lunch that very afternoon.

Percival didn't have any dingleberries now, but he doubted the bears would have been interested anyway. He sensed that something of a more meaty nature might be better suited to their taste buds' liking.

He was roughly dropped onto the hard ground, made all the harder by the various animal bones strewn across it. Percival gazed bleary-eyed into the furry face of one of his captors.

"Now hold on a second," Percival started, but the bear ignored him, stepping back with a grunt as the other two bears deposited his friends on top of him.

"You might want to give some serious consideration to what you're doing," Percival continued as he pushed a groaning Randolf off of him. Percival quickly eyed his niece and nephew, and then Tom and Roderick, to make sure they were still in one piece. They looked to be only unconscious for now, but their problems were just beginning.

"We're on a very important quest to save the Valley from ultimate evil, and I bet you'd hate to be the guys to foul that one up. Right?"

The largest bear responded with a growl and a snarl, showing off incredibly large and sharp-looking teeth. The other two beasts, who were smaller but still just as ferocious-looking, stood beside their big friend.

Tom sat up with a moan, rubbing the top of his head. "Where am I?" he asked, blinking his eyes.

"I believe it's called a den," the Bone answered. "And I wouldn't make any sudden moves if I were you."

The bears were sitting in a threatening row across from them.

"Percival?" Tom asked, his eyes growing wide as he focused on the three bears. "Who are these guys?"

"Haven't got a clue," the Bone explorer answered. "They jumped us while we were looking for you after the crash."

"I think they're bears," Roderick whispered, still lying on the floor, pretending to be unconscious.

Abbey Bone, now also awake, slowly raised her head to get a peek. "Yep, those are bears, all right," she said.

"Definitely bears," Barclay agreed, peering out from behind his sister.

"Quiet!" the big bear roared, trying to scare them into silence.

He was doing a pretty good job, but Percival didn't

want to give him the satisfaction. "Why have you brought us here?" the Bone asked.

The big bear snarled again, showing off his large, yellow teeth. "You don't ask the questions here," he said. "You're our prisoners, and we ask the questions."

Percival crossed his arms and stared at the three bears, trying not to show any fear. "So ask," he told them.

The bears looked at one another, surprised by Percival's demand.

"Go ahead," Tom spoke up. "Ask us anything. We've got nothing to hide."

Abbey, Barclay, and Roderick huddled together, nodding in agreement.

"Ask away," Abbey said.

The large bear was the first to speak. "Who are you?"

Randolf groaned aloud, finally pushing himself up into a sitting position as he returned to consciousness. "I feel like I've been struck by a bear," he grumbled, rubbing the back of his neck before turning his attention to the situation. "Oh," the Veni Yan said simply, startled by the sight before him.

"My name is Percival Bone, and these are my companions," Percival began, ignoring Randolf. "This is Tom, and beside him are my niece and nephew, Abbey and Barclay."

The two little Bones waved.

"Hello, bears," Barclay said.

"This is Roderick," Percival said, pointing to the

frightened raccoon. "And this is Randolf," the Bone finished.

The second bear, this one a little bit shorter and rounder, was next with a question. "How did you get here?"

"We came in a ship that sails the sky," Percival explained. "But a storm caused us to crash into the trees."

The last bear appeared to be dozing, his eyes half closed as he started to sway from side to side. The second bear nudged him, and he awakened with a start.

"It's ours and you can't take it from us!" the startled bear screamed.

Percival and the others were all taken aback by the outburst.

"Take what from you?" the Bone explorer asked.

"As if you didn't know," the second bear scoffed, looking to the larger beast.

"You can't fool us," the big bear said. "We know why you're here."

"Really, we don't understand," Tom said. "Tell us what you think you know."

"The honey," the big bear said, getting up from the floor and padding threateningly closer to them.

"You want to take our honey."

CHAPTER 10

Stinky and Smelly prowled around the entrance to the bears' cave.

"What should we do?" Stinky asked, leaning back on his furry haunches, nervously petting the dead squirrel he held tightly to his chest.

"Perhaps we should run as far away as possible," Smelly suggested.

"And where would we be then?" Stinky asked. "Besides, I don't think there's any place far enough away to escape the wrath of King Agak." He peered into the darkness of the cave, before turning his attention back to Smelly.

"You did see what took them, didn't you?" Smelly asked, pointing toward the entrance. "Very large bears?"

"I did see those bears," Stinky said, holding up the rotting squirrel carcass. "And so did Fredrick."

"I'm afraid of bears." Smelly began to nibble anxiously on one of his long claws.

"I'm not too fond of them either," Stinky agreed. "But if we don't help the mammals and the Bones, that leaves us alone against the King and his soldiers."

"You're right about that," Smelly said, looking back into the cave where their comrades had been taken.

"There is much more safety in numbers . . . even if those numbers include mammals and Bones."

Tom stood up, brushing dirt and bits of animal bone from his bottom.

"Honest," he said. "We're not here to steal your honey."

"Liar!" the short, round bear barked. "Why else would you be walking around the forest? Give me one good reason."

"Well, Percival here did mention our quest," Tom said, gesturing to the Bone adventurer.

"No," the shorter bear said. "You're thieves, all right. I can tell."

"And I'm telling you we're not," Tom insisted.

"The boy speaks the truth," Randolf chimed in. "We have no interest in stealing anything from you."

The larger bear squinted his brown eyes, his snout raised, sniffing the air around them as if looking for a scent that would catch them in a lie.

"Maybe you're not thieves," the big bear growled.

"Maybe you're working for them . . . for the bees."

"The bees," Tom repeated with a nod as things began to fall into place.

"Now we're working for bees?" Barclay asked, throwing up his hands. "This just keeps getting crazier by the minute!"

"C'mon, seriously," Percival asked. "You've got us all wrong. Do we look like the types who'd be working for bees?"

The big bear looked them over carefully as he considered Percival's question, and Tom saw his opportunity.

"Uh, Mister Bear, sir?" Tom called.

The bear turned his large head toward the boy. "Yeah?"

"We're not looking to steal your honey, and we're not working for the bees, honest," Tom said with all the sincerity he could muster. "But I think we're supposed to be looking for something in their hive."

The bear looked at him intently. "In the hive?" he asked. "And how were you planning to do that?"

The shorter bear reached out to grab his leader's arm. "Be careful," he said. "This could be a trap."

"Shhhhh," the larger bear said, pulling his hairy arm away. "I got this under control."

"I'm really not sure how we were going to get into the hive," Tom continued quickly. "My visions didn't show me that."

"Visions?" the bear leader asked with an odd cock to his head.

"Yeah," Tom said. "I told you, we're on this quest, and I've been having visions about where to find these pieces of the first ray of light, called the Spark. We need to gather them all so we can defeat the Nacht."

The big bear glanced at his friends. "What do you think?" he asked. The fatter bear shrugged his shoulders. "I have no idea what he's talking about, and I still don't trust them."

The third bear had nodded off again, his blocky head bobbing up and down as he snored.

"Wake him up," the large bear instructed the other.

"Hey," the short bear said, poking his comrade. "Wake up! You're doing it again."

The bear snorted and looked around, dazed. "I'm awake," he said, stifling a yawn. "Is it spring yet?"

"We're not even done with summer," the shorter bear said with a disgusted shake of his head.

"Look," Tom said as he came toward the bears, reaching into his shirt. The bear leader roared ferociously, driving him back.

"Easy. I just want to show you something," Tom said, pulling the necklace from inside his shirt. "It's made from the pieces of the Spark that we've found so far."

The big bear approached carefully, sniffing at the odd stone. "It's just a rock," he grumbled.

The other two bears had come closer for a look and a sniff.

"No, it's more than that," Tom tried to explain. "Much more."

The three bears were turning away from the boy, unimpressed, when the milky white stone started to glow. The bears gasped in unison as the Spark momentarily pulsed to life around Tom's neck, a warm yellow light that filled the dank, dark cave with something akin to sunshine.

The glow subsided as quickly as it had started, leaving the bears to stare at each other with wonder.

"Much more than just a stone," Tom told them again. "It's made from slivers of the first Spark that lit up the darkness when the Dreaming came into being." The boy rubbed the stone with his thumb as he stared at it. "We're on a quest to find all the pieces, and to stop a terrible evil from harming everyone in the Valley."

The bear leader scrutinized him. "Terrible evil?"

"It's called the Nacht," Tom explained, feeling an icy finger of dread run down his spine. "And I'd hate to think of what might happen if we don't stop it."

"The Nacht," the bear leader repeated.

"Never heard of such a thing," the chubby bear said. "I still think they're after our honey."

The other bear snored loudly.

Tom stood there with the members of his quest around him, all of them radiating a sense of purpose.

"I think I believe them," the leader said.

"What?" the short bear squawked. "What makes you think that their crazy story is true?"

"There's something about the boy," the big bear said, staring at Tom, then shifting his eyes to Randolf. "And then there's the Veni Yan. They're not likely to lie."

"So now what?" the chubby bear asked.

They were all silent for a moment, and then Tom spoke up.

"I was thinking," he began.

"Thinking about what?" the big bear asked.

"Well, since we're both looking for something that can be found inside the hive . . ."

"Yeah?" the leader encouraged.

"Maybe we could help each other," Tom suggested with a shrug.

The big bear nudged his friend's chubby gut with a furry elbow.

"I knew there was something about this kid that I liked."

Night had fallen, and the bears helped gather some wood to make a fire.

Bobby — the large bear who was obviously the leader of the three — was incredibly helpful now, even going so far as to gather some nuts and berries along with Joey and Al, the other two bears.

Well, Joey anyway, Tom observed. The bear named Al was still having a difficult time staying awake.

"So what exactly are we doing here?" Percival asked

him, dumping an armful of kindling beside the fire that Randolf was preparing.

"We're building a fire," Tom said, keeping an eye on Abbey, Barclay, and Roderick as they helped the three bears collect the wild berries that would be their supper.

"I know we're building a fire . . . but what are we *doing*?" the Bone stressed. "Remember the quest? The whole evil-taking-over-the-Valley business?"

Randolf knelt by the pile of broken branches, twigs, and dry grass, and vigorously rubbed two sticks together until there was enough heat to cause the grass to smol-der. He then bent forward, gently blowing on the smoking grass to make the flame grow.

"I think the bears can help us," Tom said.

"Ya think?" Percival asked. "Not too long ago, I thought we were going to end up as their dinner."

Tom smiled, watching Joey pointing out to the twins which berries to pick and which ones to avoid.

"I don't think they would have eaten us," Tom said.

"I'm glad you think so," Percival harrumphed as he fed the growing fire.

"The bears know where the hive is," Tom said. "And we need to find the hive." He'd removed the piece of the Spark from inside his shirt again, and rubbed his thumb along its jagged surface. "My vision showed me that another piece of the Spark is somewhere inside, and I think the bears can help us find it."

"And what will we be doing for them?" asked Randolf, who had been silent up until this point.

"That's what we need to find out," Tom said.

Just outside the entrance to the bears' den, a comfortable blaze crackled and sparked, and they were all gathered around it. Bobby and Joey sat on the ground, watching them eat, while Al had fallen over minutes ago, fast asleep.

"These berries are delicious," Roderick said, holding up one of the round, plump pieces of fruit before popping it into his mouth.

"They're called bear berries," Bobby said.

"It's what we eat when there's no honey," Joey added.

"Which is pretty much all the time these days," an unexpectedly awake Al chimed in. His eyes still looked heavy, and Tom knew that it wouldn't be long before he was snoozing again.

"You guys must really like honey," Abbey said, crunching on some of her pine nuts.

"*Like* is too soft a word," Bobby said, his eyes getting sort of glassy as he gazed into the fire.

"*Love* is much better," Joey said, thick tendrils of drool starting to run from his jowls and down his furry neck.

Bobby nodded his large, black head. "Yeah, *love* is much more appropriate. We love our honey."

Al's snoring suddenly drew all their attention, the skinnier bear having rolled onto his side, his mouth hanging open.

"What about him?" Barclay asked, pointing to the sleeping bear. "Does he love honey, too?"

"Yeah, he loves his honey, too," Joey said with a frustrated sigh.

"If he could stay awake long enough to eat it," Bobby finished.

"What's wrong with him?" Percival asked as he popped two berries into his mouth.

Joey reached over and gave his friend a poke. "His timing is all off," he explained. "He always thinks it's time to hibernate."

"Is it spring yet?" Al asked, smacking his lips and looking around dazedly.

Bobby shook his head. "We've been dealing with this problem for years. If it weren't for us, the poor slob would've probably starved to death."

"That's what friends do," Tom said, looking at the gathering around him. "You look after one another."

The bears grumbled in agreement, watching as Al drifted to sleep again.

"Sounds like his internal clock might be off," Percival

observed. "Maybe there's something I can do about that . . . after the business with the hive, of course."

This caught the attention of the bears that were still awake.

"Of course," Bobby agreed. "Now, how about that hive?"

"Where is it?" Randolf asked, picking a piece of nut from between his teeth. "Is it close by?"

"It's not too far," Joey said, turning slightly to look off into the woods. "Back that way — inside the mountain."

"How do you get inside?" Tom asked.

Bobby and Joey looked at each other.

"By going in through one of the cave openings," Bobby answered. "But those are heavily guarded by bee sentries."

"So how would you get us inside?" Tom probed.

No one said anything, and the two bears looked at each other again.

"We don't know," Joey finally confessed as he scratched his protruding belly. "We've never gotten inside before."

Bobby shook his head sadly. "The bee sentries never let us get close enough. Not to say that we haven't tried."

Joey stood up and pointed out some areas on his prominent stomach that seemed to be missing fur. "I got stung twenty-two times," he said.

"Thirty-two times," Bobby said, slowly turning his bulk around to show that he too was missing some fur from his back and bottom.

Joey reached over to swat the snoring Al, awakening him.

"How many times have you been stung?" Joey asked the bleary-eyed bear.

"Fifty-seven," Al said, covering his mouth with the back of his paw as he stifled a yawn. "And I can still feel each sting as if it happened only yesterday." He began to nod off again.

"So you've never actually been inside the hive?" Tom asked them.

"No . . . not yet," Bobby said. "But with your help . . ."

Percival slapped a hand to his forehead. "Oh boy, this should be good."

"With your help we'll get inside, and nothing will stop us," Bobby said, ignoring the Bone as he wiped the flowing saliva from his mouth with a large, furry paw. "We'll take all that we can carry. . . ."

"And then some," Joey added.

Abbey was the first to ask the question, but by the looks on the others' faces, she wasn't the only one to notice.

"Take?" she asked.

"What're you takin' out of the hive?" Barclay asked innocently.

Bobby and Joey turned to the little Bone, looking almost as if they were in some sort of trance.

"Why, honey, of course," Bobby said. "With your help, we're gonna take it all."

CHAPTER 11

Lorimar drifted through the ether, disconnected from any earthly substance, a spirit searching for a glimmer of hope.

She missed the body that she had fashioned for herself from plant, root, and rock, as she missed the friends she had made in her effort to save the Valley from the Nacht. It had been too long since Lorimar had known friendship, and she found herself momentarily distracted from her mission, wondering about the safety of her comrades.

"Hello . . . I'm here," Lorimar called out through the ghostly realm where she traveled. She could actually see her voice here, like the ripples created by a stone dropped into a calm pool of water in the forest.

Lorimar waited for a moment and was about to call out again, when she received a response.

"Help . . . us," said the voices of her people, speaking as one.

She started to follow the weak lines of sound before they could fade.

"Yes, I will help you," Lorimar said. *"But you must show me where you are."*

The ethereal world around her spirit slowly began to swirl into a whirlpool of light and color that gradually pulled her down. At first she fought it, but then the sad, sad voice came again, and she saw where she must go: down, down, down into the revolving miasma, toward its hungry black center.

She had no idea where the whirlpool would lead her, but if it would bring her closer to her people, it was a risk she was willing to take.

The darkness consumed her, and there was nothing; no sight, no sound, no up or down — only the blackness of oblivion. She almost felt herself drifting apart so that she was nearly nothing as well, but she held on.

And then, far off in the incalculable distance appeared a circle of white.

A portal . . . of light.

Lorimar flowed through the oily black, drawn by a sense of familiarity. The portal of light was small, but she surged through it, forcing her ghostly shape into another realm entirely — a realm she remembered well.

Lorimar found herself floating above a world of green, a land lush with plant life. A land that had been her home before . . .

The Dreaming sang out to her, a sad song mixed with the plaintive cries of her people — of the First Folk. She hovered above the emerald forest and then darted downward, eager to again feel the world that she loved around her.

But then she felt as if she'd hit a barrier of some kind. Stunned, she drifted above the land, realizing that an ocean of darkness surrounded her. And, as she looked closer, the darkness surrounded the Dreaming.

No, not the entire Dreaming, but a piece of it.

It was as if a portion of her wonderful world had been placed inside a bubble, floating in a sea of obsidian.

Tentatively, she floated closer, pressing herself against the invisible, yet unyielding, surface.

"Hello?" she called, desperate to know if there was someone — anyone — inside who could hear her.

"Help us!" the First Folk bellowed in response, their voices so desperate and powerful that they drove her back into the depths of the black sea.

Drifting in the ocean of pitch, she tried to understand what she had stumbled upon — a piece of her world, seemingly populated by members of her race.

How can this be? Lorimar wondered. *How is this possible?*

And then she sensed that she was no longer alone.

Something swam with her in the blackness, a presence darker than the shadows in which she floated. It was far larger than the last time she had seen it, its eyes glowing like twin fires in the night.

The Nacht.

Its gaze held her, and she waited for the inevitable attack, but it did not come. Instead, the great beast smiled, exposing rows of glistening, jagged teeth.

"Lorimar," he said, his voice like the hiss of a million snakes. "How nice of you to come."

Tom didn't like the idea of stealing from anyone . . . or *anything*.

Taking the bees' honey just didn't seem right, but they had to get inside the hive, and he doubted they'd be able to do it alone. He was left with no choice.

"I bet we can help you with that," he said to the bears.

Bobby suddenly looked as though he was baring his fangs, but Tom guessed that he was smiling.

"This is it," Joey said. "Finally!"

Bobby chuckled happily and licked his chops in anticipation. "This is gonna be great," he said. "So, how are we going to do this?"

"Nothing comes to mind right away," Tom said. "We're going to have to think about this and come up with a plan."

The bears seemed okay with this.

"You say the bees have sentries at the entrance to the hive?" Randolf asked.

"I'll say," Joey said as he rubbed the spots where he'd been stung. "If you're not a bee, you're not getting anywhere near the place."

Tom racked his brain, trying to come up with a way to get inside unharmed. According to his vision, these bees were big — he didn't want to mess with them without some sort of help. "Any ideas?" he asked, turning to Randolf.

"I know that beekeepers often use smoke as a way of calming the bees while they collect the honey," the Veni Yan priest offered.

"Smoke, you say?" Bobby questioned excitedly.

"It would have to be a lot of smoke," Joey said.

"Yeah, those hives are pretty big — and so are the bees," added Al, who was awake again.

Percival rubbed his chin, a sure sign that the Bone was thinking. "If smoke works for normal bees, more smoke should work for the bigger ones," he said.

"In theory," Randolf agreed.

"So we just have to figure out a way to fill the giant hive with a lot of smoke," Percival said matter-of-factly.

Joey got a crazy look in his eyes. "We'll set the forest on fire, and . . ."

The bear saw that his brothers were looking at him strangely and stopped.

"Burn the forest down?" Al asked, his eyelids starting to droop.

"I love honey as much as the next bear, but don't you think that's going a little bit too far?" Bobby asked.

"Sorry, I get carried away sometimes," Joey said with an embarrassed chuckle. "It's the honey — it makes me crazy."

Tom was still mulling over the facts. "Even if we could fill the hive with smoke, would the giant bees be so docile that they'd let complete strangers wander in and take whatever they want?"

"Hmm, you've got a point there, Tom," Percival agreed.

The sound of Barclay laughing distracted Tom from the moment, and he looked over to see Abbey whispering in her brother's ear. She had her hand over her mouth so that they couldn't see what she was saying, but the little boy started to laugh even harder.

"Knock it off, you two," Percival warned. "We're trying to think here."

Still laughing, Barclay raised his hand to get everyone's attention. "I have an idea," the young Bone said.

"Hey," Abbey protested, giving her brother a punch in the arm. "I thought of it, too."

Barclay continued, ignoring his sister. "So they only let bees inside the hive?" he asked.

"Yes," Bobby answered, sounding annoyed. "Only bees."

"If they only let bees in . . ." Barclay began.

Abbey leaned over and put her hand over her brother's mouth.

"Then we have to turn into bees," she finished for him.

All around the campfire went silent, all eyes on the twins.

"Pretend to be bees?" Bobby asked, a look of confusion on his furry face.

"Yeah, you know, pretend," Barclay said, getting up and running around the fire. Abbey got up as well, and went in the opposite direction.

"Bzzzzzzzzzzzzzzzz! Bzzzzzzzzzzzzzzzz!" Barclay said. "I'm a bee — where's all the honey? Bzzzzzzzzzzzzzzzzzzz!"

"Bzzzzzzzzzzzzz! Bzzzzzzzzzzzzz!" Abbey buzzed. "I used to be a Bone, but now I'm a bee. Bzzzzzzzzzzzzzzzzzzz!"

"I don't think that would work," Roderick chimed in. "You don't even look like bees."

The twins began to laugh again, and pretty soon they were all laughing, until Al suddenly came awake, blood-shot eyes bulging, nose pointed in the air.

"Intruders," the bear growled, and his brothers began to sniff the air, too.

"He's right," Joey said. "We're not alone."

Bobby rose to his feet and headed for a section of forest nearby.

"I smell something dead," the bear growled, picking up speed as he ran toward a thick section of underbrush. "And something that stinks worse."

The bushes began to tremble as Bobby stopped in front of them.

"I know you're in there," the bear said menacingly. "Come out before I come in. You won't like what happens if I have to come in."

The bushes rustled again violently as a familiar voice drifted out from the leaves.

"I'm not going out there," said the voice. "There are bears out there."

"But we have to," said another equally familiar voice. "We've been discovered."

Tom quickly rose and walked toward Bobby and the bushes.

"It's all right, Bobby," he said. "They're with us."

The great bear snarled ferociously. "I know that smell and they're not with you," he said, rising to stand on his hind legs. Joey and Al joined him, doing their best to be scary.

"No, really, they're with us," Tom insisted. He turned to the bushes. "I think you should come out now, guys," he said.

"Is that you, mammal?" Smelly asked.

"Yes, it's me," he said. "Both of you come out of there right now."

The two Rat Creatures parted the bushes, sticking their hairy faces out into the open. All three of the bears began to growl, their fur bristling at the sight of the Rats.

·Chapter 12·

The *Queen of the Sky* creaked and moaned, gently bobbing up and down as it lay nestled in the boughs of the forest trees, caressed by the morning winds.

"This place is a mess!" Abbey proclaimed from the hold of the sky ship.

"Don't worry about that," Barclay said, carefully moving across the creaking floor, the ship's up-and-down movement making it feel like they were sailing on the ocean. "We just need to find Uncle Percy's tools so he can get working on that smoker."

"Where did you put them?" Roderick asked from atop a wooden box.

"Well, they're certainly not where I put them now," Abbey said, nearly overwhelmed by how the hold looked since setting down in the forest trees. "I don't know where to begin."

"Start somewhere," Barclay said, holding on to the side of a crate as the *Queen* dipped down, the tree limbs protesting its weight. "Everybody is waiting for us."

Abbey moved some small boxes aside to see what might have fallen behind them. Roderick squeezed into the corner, where Abbey couldn't quite fit, for a peek. "Nothing that looks like tools back here."

"I don't know what they're in such a hurry for. We still haven't figured out how we're gonna get into the hive without the bees attacking," Abbey complained.

"Don't you worry about that," Barclay said as he climbed over some boxes marked MOTOR PARTS. "I'm coming up with a plan."

What remained of their potatoes had overturned, and Abbey squatted down to place them back in their storage box. Roderick watched her hungrily.

"You're coming up with a plan?" she asked, stifling a laugh. "This should be good."

"Go ahead and laugh," Barclay said. A crate of materials used for repairing holes in the *Queen*'s balloons had broken open. "You won't be the only smarty-pants once I figure out what we're going to do."

"How's that coming?" she asked.

"I don't have anything yet," the little boy admitted. Roderick had scampered over to help him, and they were both now lugging an armful of colorful silk material and tossing it aside to see what was beneath it. "But I think I'm getting close."

Abbey watched as the slippery fabric slid across the floor, noticing the pretty colors. There was blue and green, yellow and black. . . .

Yellow and black.

Abbey Bone's brain grabbed hold of the germ of an idea. . . . It had started off as a silly joke by the campfire last night, and was becoming something a whole lot bigger.

"I got it," she said, an excited smile forming as she thought the idea through.

"The tools?" Roderick asked.

"Nope," she said, turning toward her brother and her raccoon friend. "I think I know how we're gonna get inside that hive."

Randolf could hear the song of the giant bees in the early morning air, even though he was still a good distance away from the hive.

He and Bobby carefully moved toward the sound of the humming, using the many trees and bushes of the forest as cover.

"That's close enough," the large bear said as softly as his powerful voice was able.

Randolf stopped, squatting and reaching out to peer through a wall of thick ferns at what lay ahead.

To say that the Veni Yan was impressed was an understatement.

The giant bees had made their home inside a mountain cave, not unlike the one inhabited by the bears. Bees came and went through the entrance, while the sentries buzzed nearby, guarding the opening against intruders.

Randolf studied the mountain above the cave, his keen eyes searching . . . searching. . . . And then he found it: a large, jagged crack farther up in the mountain's side.

"There," he said, pointing toward the opening. "That is where the smoke should be applied."

Bobby craned his massive neck to see. "Nice," he growled. "High up. Not too heavily watched. I like it."

"The smoke should filter down into the cave, and into the hive, neutralizing the workers. If we act swiftly, Tom will be able to find the piece of the Spark."

"The Spark?" Bobby questioned with an edge.

Randolf looked at the bear. "Yes, the Spark," he said calmly, as was the tone of the Veni Yan. "We are on a quest to protect this valley from evil, or have you forgotten that?"

"Hrrrmph," the big bear grumbled. "I didn't forget. But as far as I'm concerned, the honey comes first."

Randolf felt a flash of annoyance. "I don't think you understand the importance of our mission. This evil, like a thick black fog, is spreading, claiming any and all that it touches. I hear tell that even the Dragons have fallen to this threat."

"Dragons?" Bobby asked, more serious now.

Randolf nodded slowly, driving his point home. "Dragons."

"But we're talking about honey here," Bobby whined. He licked his chops. "And not just any honey . . . the tastiest honey in all the Valley!"

"Honey that won't matter to you or anybody else if the Nacht achieves his nefarious goals," Randolf warned. "The Nacht will take it all from you . . . your honey, your brothers, the Valley . . . and perhaps the world beyond it."

Bobby looked at him. "My brothers?" he asked.

Randolf nodded again. "Everything that matters will cease to be if the world is plunged into darkness."

Bobby rubbed his hairy chin with a large paw. "That isn't good."

"No, it's not," Randolf agreed. "And that is why you and your brothers must help us — help Tom — find this newest piece of the Spark."

"This Tom, he's pretty special, huh?"

With the question put to him, Randolf didn't know how to respond. He had seen things that made him think that perhaps . . . perhaps the Dreaming knew what it was doing in choosing the boy.

But then again, perhaps not.

"I hope that he is, for if he isn't . . . we are all doomed."

The bear was quiet for a moment, staring out through their cover at the hive, deep in thought.

"You're right," Bobby said. "No sense in having the tastiest honey in the whole Valley if you can't enjoy it."

"Indeed."

"I suppose this quest of yours should move to the top of the list," the big bear sighed, as if the notion had just come to him.

"That's a very good idea," Randolf agreed.

The bear smiled, showing off his big yellow teeth. "That's why I'm the boss," he said with a wink.

"Let's get back to the cave and tell the others that we've found where the smoke will go," Randolf said, heading back into the forest. "And hopefully, in our absence someone has come up with a way for us to get in and out of the hive safely."

There was a lot of noise coming from the back of the cave.

Tom was trying to stay focused on what Percival was doing in front of him, but Abbey and Barclay were working with the Bears on some sort of secret plan.

To say he was a bit nervous was an understatement.

"So what do you call this again?" Tom asked, trying to distract himself from the voices and growls drifting out from where he could not see. He was sitting with Roderick and Percival as the Bone toiled on the contraption that was supposed to pump smoke into the giant bees' hive.

"It's called a smoker," the Bone said as he fiddled with a swinging metal door on the front of the barrel-sized device. "You burn stuff down here in the belly of the beast, and the smoke comes out from" — Percival picked up a piece of metal piping — "here, as soon as I get it attached."

Tom watched the Bone work. "I still can't believe you had everything you needed to build this thing on board the *Queen*."

Percival reached down to grab a wrench and went back to work. "Well, I like to be prepared for just about any situation, and stock the *Queen* accordingly. Besides, it's not like we're talking about a complex piece of machinery here." He leaned back to admire his work. "One more screw and that should do it," he said, wiping some sweat from his brow.

Roderick, his little raccoon hands filled with screws, handed one to Percival.

"It's a good thing I had this old stove on board," the Bone added, referring to the metal shell that made up the smoker's body. He took the final screw from the raccoon and finished attaching the pipe to the smoker. "Almost removed it from the *Queen* after my last adventure south of Boneville, but I just never got around to it. Pretty lucky, I'd say."

"Or maybe the Dreaming thought you'd need it," Roderick suggested.

Tom looked at the raccoon. "You think?"

The raccoon shrugged. "The Dreaming seems pretty smart. It brought us all together, didn't it?"

An argument had broken out from the back of the

cave. Barclay Bone yelled something, followed by an Abbey Bone retort.

"So, what are they up to again?" Tom asked.

Roderick shook his head. "They wouldn't tell me, said they wanted to surprise everyone with how smart they are."

The argument got even louder, Abbey's and Barclay's voices reaching a fevered crescendo loud enough to even wake up the two sleeping Rat Creatures in the corner.

"Can't you keep it down?" Stinky asked. "We're trying to rest up here."

"Yes," Smelly agreed. "We're going to need all our wits about us if we're going to steal honey or sparks or whatever it is we're supposed to be doing."

Tom ignored the beasts, knowing that they'd be back to snoring in a matter of minutes.

Abbey came stomping around the corner with a look on her face that could've curdled milk.

"Uh-oh," Percival said, looking up from his work. "This isn't going to be pretty." He quickly went back to the smoker.

"Hey, Abbey," Tom said in his most friendly voice. "Everything all right?"

She looked at him with fire in her eyes.

"No," she said. "No, it's not."

"What's wrong?" Roderick asked.

"It's that stupid brother of mine, and those stupid bears," she roared. "They won't let me help with anything and it was my idea . . . well, at least half of it anyway."

She looked back toward the cave. "I bet those bears think he's smarter than I am," the little Bone fumed.

Tom saw that this could go in a bad direction, so he tried to calm Abbey down. "I don't think it has anything to do with who's smarter," he said.

She glared at him. "Then why won't they listen to me?" she snapped.

Tom wasn't exactly sure what to say, not wanting to make the situation worse. "Uh . . . help me out here, Roderick," he begged.

Abbey turned her hard stare on the raccoon, her tiny arms folded across her chest.

"Ummm," Roderick stammered. "Ahhhh, it's probably nothing personal, it's . . . ahhhhhh . . . maybe they just like Barclay better than you."

The little girl looked as though she'd been hit in the face with a mud ball.

"Good one, Roderick," Percival said quietly as he continued to put the finishing touches on the smoker.

Abbey's face twisted up, her lower lip beginning to tremble, and then she started to sob.

"Nice job, Roderick," Tom said to his furry friend.

"What?" Roderick cried as Abbey ran out of the

cave in tears. "I was just trying to help!"

"Percival," Tom called. "Maybe you should —"

"Busy with the smoker here," the Bone said. He'd picked up a hammer and started to bang on the hard metal surface.

Tom turned to Roderick, and the little raccoon threw up his hands. "I'm helping Percival," he said, grabbing a tool with his paw. "And besides, she punches really hard."

"Fine, I'll talk to her," Tom said, getting to his feet.

"She really likes you," Percival offered.

"Watch out for her right hook," Roderick warned.

Tom shook his head and stepped from the cave. "Abbey?" he called, not seeing the little Bone. "Abbey, where are you?"

He heard her soft crying nearby and, following the sound, found her huddled in the rotted-out stump of a tree, face buried in her hands. Tom stood there for a moment, not knowing what to do.

"Hey," he said finally.

She didn't acknowledge him, and continued to sob.

"Umm," he began. "You're going to get your dress dirty sitting in there," he said, just to have something to say.

"I don't care," Abbey sobbed. "This dress is stupid and so am I."

He squatted down in front of her. "That's not true." He picked up a stick and began to poke the ground with it. "You're really smart, and everybody knows it."

"Everybody except those dumb bears," she sniffled.

"No, I think they know it, too," he said as he drew squiggly lines in the dirt.

She looked at him, her eyes red and swollen. "You think?" she asked uncertainly.

Tom nodded. "I really do. Didn't you come up with half the idea that you guys are working on?"

"Uh-huh," she said, wiping her nose.

"See, Barclay didn't come up with the whole idea by himself — he needed you."

"Yeah," she agreed, the tears stopping. "There wouldn't even be an idea without me."

Tom smiled, glad that she wasn't crying anymore. "So don't think anybody thinks you're dumb, Abbey. You're a very important part of our team."

"And you'd be lost without me?" she asked excitedly.

"Yup, we'd be lost without you."

She shot up from the tree stump and wrapped her tiny arms around Tom's neck in a big hug. "Thanks, Tommy," she said, squeezing him tight.

Tom laughed self-consciously as he tentatively returned her hug. He was reminded of his little sister, Lottie, and how much he missed her.

A familiar voice called out then.

"Hey, Abbey!" It was Barclay.

Tom and Abbey turned to see Barclay, Al, and Joey standing outside the cave entrance. Roderick was there, too.

"Go on, say it," the raccoon urged, poking Barclay in the arm.

"Ummm, Abbey, we're sorry that we drove you away," he apologized.

"Yeah," Joey said. He elbowed Al, who was starting to drift off to sleep. "Your turn," the bear said.

Al snorted and looked around. "Oh," he said, remembering what he needed to do.

"Sorry, Abbey," he said in his gruff bear voice. "We need your help."

Abbey charged off in the direction of the cave. "I accept your apologies," she said. "I knew you guys wouldn't be able to get it done without me."

Tom chuckled as he followed, watching the Bone twins and the two bears return to the cave, and their super-secret project.

"Did you make them come out here?" Tom asked Roderick.

"Yeah," the raccoon said. "They said they were stuck and that they needed Abbey to help them. I told them the only way that would happen is if they all went outside and apologized to her."

"Thanks," Tom said, patting the raccoon on the head.

"No problem," Roderick replied. "I just want to see what it is they're working on."

"You and me both."

The anticipation was growing.

Tom straightened as Barclay came out, thinking they were ready, but the Bone went over to the Rat Creatures, woke them up, and motioned for them to follow him to the back of the cave.

Now Tom was really confused. *What in the world could they be doing with the Rat Creatures?* he wondered. Percival and Roderick looked just as puzzled.

"Before you ask, I haven't got a clue," Percival said with an amused shake of his head.

"Here's Randolf and Bobby now," Roderick announced.

Tom turned just as the Veni Yan and large bear were entering the cave.

"You're just in time," Tom said to them.

"For?" the priest asked.

"I guess Abbey and Barclay have come up with a way for us to get inside the hive," Tom explained.

"Have they, now?" Randolf responded. He folded his arms. "This should be interesting."

"How are they planning we do that?" Bobby asked.

Tom shrugged. "I haven't any idea," he said. "But I guess they're going to show us."

"Hrrrm," the big bear said, brow furrowed in curious thought. Tom knew exactly how he was feeling.

Roderick scampered back from the far end of the cave.

"I told them everybody's here," the raccoon said. He quickly sat down on the ground. "They said we should prepare to be amazed. I can't wait."

And it was then that the twins appeared.

"Is everybody here?" Abbey asked.

"Looks to be," Barclay answered her.

It was good to see the twins standing together without hitting each other, Tom thought, as he awaited the big revelation.

"Okay," Abbey said, barely able to contain her excitement. "Remember the other night around the campfire when you guys were saying how the bees only let bees into the hive? And then I said —"

"We said," Barclay protested.

"*We* said you should pretend to be bees?" Abbey finished.

Tom and everybody else nodded, remembering.

"So this is how we're going to do it," Abbey said, her eyes so wide that they looked as though they might pop from her head.

"We're gonna change into bees," Barclay said, turning toward the shadows behind them. "C'mon out, guys!"

Four giant bees came running into the room.

"Buzz! Buzz!" said one.

"Bzzzzzzzzzzzzz!" said another, as it twirled in a circle.

"I think I will go and make some honey," the third said, before tripping and falling to the ground.

"Get up, Al," Joey's distinctive voice said. "Bees don't roll around on the ground."

Within seconds the giant bee — Al — was snoring, with the other giant bee — Joey — trying to get him up. The other two — the Rat Creatures — were running around in circles, buzzing.

Tom couldn't believe what he was seeing.

"You've made bee costumes," Percival said, the first to speak up.

Barclay and Abbey nodded vigorously. "Aren't they great?" the twins asked.

Tom glanced over to Randolf and saw that the Veni Yan warrior's eyes were emotionless as he stared at the players in their costumes.

"This is their plan?" the priest asked.

"This is it," Tom answered.

"Those costumes wouldn't fool a child, never mind a hive of bees," Randolf said.

Tom was about to agree when he happened to glance over at Bobby, expecting a similar look of disbelief from the bear, but instead he saw something else entirely.

Bobby's eyes were wide, his mouth moving as he tried to speak.

"What's wrong, Bobby?" Tom asked, worried.

"Giant . . . giant . . . bees," the large bear said, and Tom realized that he was afraid.

Tom gave Randolf a look before approaching the bear. "It's all right, Bobby," Tom said. "Those really aren't giant bees."

"They're . . . they're not?" the bear asked fearfully. "But they look . . ."

"Show 'em, guys," Barclay called to the bees, and one after another they removed their headpieces, antennae made from stiff pieces of rope that bobbed about.

"Well?" Joey asked, as he held his bee mask beneath his arm. "What do you think?" He waved at the others with a flourish.

Bobby jumped back, clutching at his chest in surprise.

"Are you kidding me?" Percival whispered to Tom. "Those are the worst bee costumes I've ever seen."

"Shhh," Tom told him.

"Those are supposed to be bees?" Roderick asked, confused, and Randolf brought a hand to his mouth to cover the smile that threatened to appear.

"I could probably fix them up a bit if you —" Percival began.

"No," Bobby commanded, holding up a large paw, silencing the Bone.

"Al, you asked me what I thought?" he said to his brother.

Everybody was silent, eager to hear what Bobby had to say.

"I think we're soon going to have more honey than we know what to do with."

The bear brothers started to cheer wildly, as did Abbey and Barclay, and Tom found himself a little less enthused for the mission ahead of them, and quite a bit more worried.

The Constable was not happy. They had yet to stumble across the wreckage of the sky ship, and their Rat Creature comrades were growing irritated at the lack of progress.

He stood in the shadows of the forest and scanned the treetops. He'd expected to have found something by now, some sign of the shattered craft driven from the sky by the storm that he and his brethren had conjured.

"Well?" Agak demanded, coming to stand menacingly beside him.

"Nothing yet," the Constable said. "But soon. I can sense it."

"Soon. Soon. And more soon," the Rat King snarled. "That is what you say, but you still give us nothing."

The Constable turned to look at the other Rats. "One must have patience," he said calmly. "Think of it as a game."

"A game?" Agak questioned.

"Yes, a game. You Rats play games, don't you?" the possessed man asked the beast.

"Chew the limbs off your enemies is a good game," King Agak replied with a toothy snarl.

"Yes," the Constable agreed. "I'm sure it is."

"This is not as much fun," Agak continued with a shake of his furry head.

"Not yet," the Constable said. "But if we all have patience, eventually, it will be."

The Rat King seemed to think about this. "Soon?" he asked.

"Soon," the Constable replied with a nod.

There was a commotion from somewhere in the woods, and the Constable drew his short sword.

One of the King's soldiers bounded from the cover of the forest with something dangling from its enormous maw.

"What is this?" the Constable asked as the beast grew near.

He extended a hand toward the Rat and it hissed menacingly, drawing back.

"Silence!" Agak ordered, and his soldier cowered at the command.

The Constable approached the animal and took a piece of fabric from its mouth. He smiled as he examined the torn cloth. It was from the sky craft's balloons, and he knew that the ship wouldn't have been able to stay aloft for long with a punctured balloon.

He held it out to the Rat King. "Soon," he repeated, rubbing the material between his thumb and finger.

"Soon," King Agak replied, his jagged smile wide enough to split his face.

CHAPTER 13

Percival tensed at the sound of bees buzzing overhead. He, the twins, and Roderick were in the back of a four-wheeled cart that they'd retrieved from the belly of the *Queen*. Abbey, Barclay, and Roderick were keeping the smoker steady as Al pulled them up the side of the mountain. Percival worked on a little something that might help the sleepy bear with his problem.

The cart lurched to a stop as the humming grew louder. The Bone explorer reached up through the covering of branches and leaves that had been woven as camouflage over the moving cart and peeked up at the sky.

A swarm of giant yellow and black bees flew overhead on their way to the hive.

"You okay out there, Al?" Percival called softly.

The bear was also camouflaged, his head and body covered in a suit of twigs and leaves. He was fast asleep.

Percival sighed, carefully sliding from the back of the cart and over to the bear. He'd brought along the item that he'd been tinkering with.

"Hey, Al," Percival said, giving the bear's furry side a poke with his shoe. "Wake up."

Al came awake, looking around before his eyes focused on the Bone.

"Guess I dozed off again, huh?" the bear said.

"Yeah," the Bone confirmed. "But I think I've got something here that might help you out."

"What is it?" the bear asked suspiciously.

"Well, it started out as an old alarm clock," the Bone explained. "But I've rigged it in such a way so that every time you doze off, the bells will ring and wake you up."

"Really?" Al asked, liking the idea.

Percival had attached a length of rope to the modified alarm clock, and Al bent down so he could put it over his head.

"See, you wear it around your neck, like this," he said. The device was high up on Al's chest, and there were some thick wires that formed a kind of hammock that rested beneath his chin.

"What's this for?" the bear asked, poking at the thick wire.

"When you start to fall asleep, your chin will push down on the wire and make the bells ring. Give it a try."

Al lowered his furry chin and made the alarm go off.

"What do you think?" Percival asked, happy that his invention seemed to be working.

"I think this is great," the bear grumbled. "Thank you."

Percival patted the bear's leg. "Glad to help."

Barclay and Abbey stuck their heads out from underneath the camouflaged tarp. "Everything all right, Uncle Percy?" Barclay asked.

"We're good," Percival said, returning to the cart. "We just had to wait for that swarm of bees to pass over, but we're ready to go now. Right, Al?"

"Right," the bear said, grabbing the wagon's handle in his powerful jaws. Percival climbed back into the cart, checking to make sure the smoker was still secure — he didn't want it falling on any of the little guys.

"The smoke ain't gonna hurt the bees, is it, Uncle Percy?" Abbey asked.

"Not at all, Abs," Percival reassured her as the wagon lurched forward, and they were on their way up the mountainside again. "The smoke just makes them kinda dopey."

"Dopey like Barclay?" she teased with a giggle.

"I'll give you dopey," the little boy Bone said, shaking his fist. "If it wasn't for me being a genius, we never would've been able to get into the hive and . . ."

"Here we go again," Roderick said, putting his paws over his eyes.

"If you're a genius, I'm a monkey's uncle!" Abbey screamed, bending around her uncle to see her twin brother. "I'm the one that helped make the costumes so realistic!"

"All right, you two," Uncle Percival warned.

"There wouldn't even be any costumes if I hadn't come up with the idea first," Barclay countered.

"I'm not gonna say this again," Percival said wearily.

"I'm the one who said . . ." Abbey continued.

Percival was fed up. "If you two don't stop bickering this minute, I'll . . ." He paused, desperately trying to think of something. "If you don't stop bickering . . . as soon as we're done here, I'll take you both back to Boneville," he finished.

There was instant silence in the back of the cart.

"How . . . how are you gonna do that, Uncle Percy?" Barclay asked, his voice uncertain.

"Don't test me," Percival warned with a shake of his finger. "I'll repair the *Queen of the Sky* so fast you two won't know what hit you. You'll be back in Boneville before you know it, and there'll be no quest for either of you."

The cart rocked back and forth, steadily climbing the mountain. Percival watched the twins from the corner of his eye and saw them look at each other. For a moment, he thought they might start arguing again, but they remained quiet.

The cart came to another stop, and Percival again peered through the camouflaged cover. "Are we here?" he asked Al, who was admiring the alarm device around his neck.

"We're here," the bear said. "Be careful getting out," he warned. "We're on a slant."

Percival cautiously climbed out of the cart, his boots sending a mini avalanche of small pebbles down the mountain.

Al was placing two large rocks behind each of the cart's wheels to keep it from rolling backward. "That oughta keep it steady," the bear said, helping Percival to throw back the camouflaged cover.

"Excellent," Percival said.

He took a quick look around, surveying the sky to be sure they didn't have any unwelcome guests. When he saw that all was clear, Percival helped the twins and Roderick out of the cart, and reached for the smoker.

"Where are we going with this?" he asked the bear as he loosened the ropes that held the metal container in place.

"Should be right up there a ways." Al motioned with his head to farther up the mountain while he helped Percival haul the smoker from the cart.

"You got your end all right?" Percival asked.

"Got it," the bear grunted.

Percival allowed the twins and Roderick to help them

up the incline by supporting the long metal pipe that would send the smoke down into the cave.

"Careful, dummy," Abbey said to her brother as he slipped on some loose rocks.

"I'm no dummy, you stupid —"

"You'll be back in Boneville before you know it," Percival warned, and they immediately fell silent.

Al and Percival carefully set the smoker down next to the jagged opening in the mountainside. "This looks like the spot Bobby was talking about," the bear said.

Percival knelt down and cautiously stuck his head into the opening in the mountain. He wished he had the flashlight he'd traded away at the marketplace, for it was pitch dark inside and he couldn't see a thing.

"Are you sure we can reach the hive from here?" Percival asked.

Al stuck his head inside the opening, and Percival could hear him inhale sharply.

"The hive is down there, all right," Al said with a goofy grin. "And so is the honey . . . lots and lots of honey." The bear started to drool, thick strings of spit trailing from the corners of his mouth.

"Ew!" Abbey exclaimed, wrinkling her nose.

"I love bears, I really do, but that's just gross," Barclay added.

The bear wiped at his mouth with his paws. "Sorry about that. Sometimes I get a little overexcited."

"That's all right, Al," Roderick said compassionately. "Sometimes I drool in my sleep."

"Everything good?" Al asked, as the Bone made sure that the smoker was stable, adjusting the pipe and positioning the nozzle at its end so that it pointed inside the cave.

"Perfect," he said, giving the bear the thumbs-up.

Al went back to the cart, then returned with a basket of dried moss, leaves, and pieces of old branches in his mouth and set them down in front of Percival and the kids. "This should do it."

"Looks it," Percival said. "Seems nice and dry — should make a fine smoke."

He opened the hatch in the belly of the smoker, and he and the twins and Roderick began stuffing the moss and leaves inside.

"I should be getting back," Al said, as he turned toward the cart.

Percival left the remainder of the loading to the kids and joined the bear as he pulled the rocks from behind the cart's wheels.

"Do you remember your lines?" he asked the bear with a smile.

"Buzz? Buzz?" Al asked.

"Excellent," Percival said. "If I had my eyes closed, I'd swear there was a giant bee around here."

Al smiled a big bear grin. "Well, I have been practicing," he said, as if letting Percival in on a big secret. "Thanks again." He glanced down to the alarm device beneath his chin.

"Don't mention it," Percival said. "And good luck."

Then off Al went, back down the mountain with the cart, as Percival turned toward the twins and Roderick.

"So," he asked, rubbing his hands together. "Who wants to make some smoke?"

Hunkered down in the woods near the cave that would lead them to the hive, Tom watched as Randolf donned his bee costume.

"I had no idea that we would be wearing these . . . outfits as well," the Veni Yan priest said with obvious distaste.

Tom knew how he felt, but if they were all going into the hive, then they would all need to look the part.

"We have to fool them," Tom explained.

"These wouldn't fool —"

"Randolf, stop," Tom said, feeling guilty and a little bit afraid as the words left his mouth. The warrior priest glared at him.

"This is what needs to be done," Tom said with as much

authority as he could muster. "If wearing bee costumes will get us inside the hive, then so be it."

"But we don't know if it will work," Randolf pointed out.

"Oh, it'll work," Bobby stressed as he carefully slipped his large, hairy legs into the black sleeves that were supposed to imitate the bees' many limbs. "I can't believe you have any doubt," he said, pulling the yellow and black striped body of the costume over his large, protruding gut. "Look at us." He motioned toward Joey, who was already in his costume. "We're not bears anymore, we're bees."

Tom really couldn't see it. To him they looked like bears and Rat Creatures wearing horrible bee costumes, but he didn't have the heart to say anything.

"But what if the bees should see through our disguises?" Randolf asked. It was a good question, and a possibility that Tom didn't want to think about at the moment.

"Then we'll be stung," Stinky spoke up with a fearful gulp, half in and half out of his costume.

"Repeatedly," Smelly added, and Tom could have sworn that he saw tears in the Rat's eyes.

"I wouldn't worry," Joey reassured them. "The bees will be so dazed from the smoke that they won't be thinking clearly."

Tom turned his attention to the bees above as they dropped out of the sky and into the cave opening. They were even larger than his vision had shown, and he was sure he didn't want to risk being on the receiving end of those stingers.

"I don't think we should do this," Randolf said firmly.

"What do you mean?" Bobby asked, already wearing his bee head.

"Yeah," Joey asked. "We can't pull out now. We're so close."

Tom knew how crazy the plan was, and how foolish they all looked, but it didn't change the fact that they needed to get into that hive.

Randolf looked at him then. "You're our leader, boy," Randolf stated, standing there dressed as a bee. "Does this seem wise to you?"

Tom swallowed hard, understanding the warrior's frustrations but knowing that they were all out of options.

"We should proceed as planned," the boy said.

"But —" Randolf started to object.

"We don't have time to argue!" Tom said, a little caught off guard by his own outburst. He reached beneath his costume, gripped the piece of solidified light, and removed it for all to see. "Another fragment is inside that hive," Tom said. "My visions have shown me that . . . and we need that piece."

Randolf looked like he still might have something else to say, so Tom pressed his point. "We don't have much time left."

Randolf stared at him, and Tom stared right back.

"I hope you're right about this," the Veni Yan priest sighed, placing his headpiece and antennae onto his head.

"We'll be fine," Tom said reassuringly, putting his own headgear on, and hoping he was right. For the fate of the Valley — and more — was depending on them.

Percival lit a match and touched the flame to the pile of dried forest stuff that had been loaded into the belly of the makeshift smoker.

"Here goes nothing," he said, dropping the match inside and quickly closing the door.

The twins and Roderick scrambled close to the opening in the side of the mountain, waiting for the results. It wasn't long before wisps of thick gray smoke began to trail from the end of the smoker's pipe and into the cave.

"There it goes, Uncle Percy," Abbey said, excited.

"Those bees won't know what hit 'em," Barclay added.

"How long do you think it will take, Percival?" Roderick asked.

The Bone moved closer to the opening, to see how the smoke was progressing. There was a downdraft inside, and it was sucking the smoke into the cave as quickly as it was made.

"At this rate, not long at all," he said. He glanced over at the pile of material that they still had to burn, and realized they might need more. "Got a job for you kids." He picked up some of the leaves and moss from the pile. "We'll need more fuel for the smoker. Think you can find some more stuff like this for me?"

The three were gone in an instant. It was good to give them something to do — anything to keep them from fighting.

The bee guards patrolling the interior chambers of the hive were the first to notice the smoke. Usually when they sensed a threat, they would release a chemical-like aroma into the air, alerting the others in the hive.

But this smoke had the strangest effect on the sentry bees — it took away their defensive response. And without that, the smoke was allowed to flow through the hive, calming the great bees.

And making it easier for the hive to be infiltrated.

Tom could have sworn that he heard the sound of bells ringing as Al emerged from the woods behind them.

"I'm back," Al said as he dropped the handle of the cart he was dragging.

"Did you get Percival and the kids up the mountain all right?" Tom asked.

"Yep. They had the smoker set up and ready to go when I left."

"Nothing yet," Joey said. He was watching the mouth of the cave through the thick vegetation.

Bobby dragged Al's costume over to him. "Get into this fast. As soon as we see smoke, we're moving in."

Tom's nerves were still frazzled. "Should we go over the plan one more time?" he asked, wanting to be sure that they'd thought of everything.

Randolf remained silent, Tom already well aware of how he was feeling.

"We've already gone over this," Bobby said, exasperated. "As soon as we see the smoke, we go in, we pretend to be bees, and you and the Veni Yan — wheeling the cart — stay close to us. We grab all the honey we can and then —"

Randolf cleared his throat, glaring at the bear.

"Oh, right . . . you find the piece of the Spark you're looking for, and then we grab all the honey, and we head back to our cave as fast as we can."

An alarm bell suddenly sounded and they all looked around, startled by the jangling sound. They looked over to see Al adjusting something strange around his neck.

"What's that?" Bobby wanted to know.

"Something that Percival made for me," the bear explained. "It wakes me up if I fall asleep."

Tom had to smile. That Percival Bone was pretty amazing, and a real benefit to the mission. They were very lucky to have him.

Al approached the larger bear, his headpiece slightly askew. "Now I can really help. How do I look?" he asked, his voice muffled by the mask.

"Like a bee fresh from the hive," Bobby said as he reached out to straighten Al's head.

"Hey, guys!" Joey called out.

Tom's heart began to hammer in his chest as he turned his attention to the smallest of the bears. Joey was holding some of the wild foliage aside to give them all a view of the cave entrance. Plumes of gray smoke billowed out and the smell of burning vegetation filled the air.

"It's time," Joey said.

And at last they were ready, moving toward the cave as one — a swarm of their own.

CHAPTER 14

Pulling the cart behind them, Tom and Randolf followed the bears and the two Rats toward the mouth of the cave.

"Are you ready for this, boy?" Randolf asked.

Tom hesitated a moment. "Truthfully?"

The Veni Yan chuckled. "We should remember our purpose here, and who we serve," he said calmly. "Trust in the guidance of the Dreaming."

"How about me?" Tom asked the warrior. "Do you trust me?"

Randolf looked at the boy, his face emotionless. "Ask me again if we get out of this in one piece," he said.

"Fair enough," Tom said. He was ready, but still eager to have this part of their quest completed.

Bobby led the troupe to the cave, and they all tensed as they passed the intimidating bee sentries. The bees stared at them with their large, bulbous eyes — seeing, but not really. The smoke was doing its job, making the normally aggressive guardians docile. Once inside the cave, Bobby paused and turned to his comrades. Tom could see that the big bear was afraid.

"Remember, we're bees," Tom said, nodding his head and making the rope antennae bounce up and down. This seemed to give the bear the courage he needed, and they all followed him through the billowing smoke and farther into the cave.

Tom held his breath as he passed through the shifting curtain of gray, blinking his eyes furiously against the burning haze.

A low, menacing buzz suddenly filled the air, and two guard bees headed up the passage to confront them.

"Our first test," Randolf said quietly.

Tom felt an ache in his chest, and realized he was still holding his breath. Slowly he exhaled.

The guard bees went right up to the costumed Bobby.

"Bzzzz!" Bobby said, wiggling his body in such a way that made his fake wings of cloth flap. "Bzzzzzzz! Bzzzzzzzz! Bzzzz! Bzzzz!" He turned to his brothers and the Rats, motioning for them to do the same.

"Bzzzzzzzzzzz! Buzz! Buzz!" Joey said.

"Bzzzzzzzzzzzzzzzzzzzzzzzzzzzzz!" Al joined in enthusiastically, managing to stay awake.

"Uh," said Smelly. "Buzz?"

Stinky cleared his throat first. "Ahem! Buzz! Buzzy! Buzz! Buzz!"

Then Tom noticed the Rat seemed to be fishing around inside his costume.

"What's he doing?" Tom asked. He didn't have a good feeling about this.

Randolf watched with a cautious eye. "I have no idea."

Smelly withdrew Fredrick, and he, too, was wearing a tiny bee costume.

"Buzz! Buzz! Buzz!" the Rat creature said in a squeaky voice, making the costumed dead squirrel pretend to fly in the air.

"Knock that off!" Smelly said in a furious whisper, elbowing his partner in his gut.

"What?" Stinky asked in surprise. "I didn't think it would be right for Fredrick to be left out, so I used some of my costume to make —"

"Quiet!" Smelly ordered, and turned his attention back to the real bees. Randolf and Tom slowly moved closer, pulling the cart behind them.

The guard bees seemed to be studying the odd bees that had come into their hive. Then after what seemed like an eternity, they moved aside and allowed the group to pass.

"If I hadn't seen it with my own eyes . . ." Randolf said to Tom as they hurried along behind the Rats, who were following the bears.

Tom tried not to look at the sentries as they passed through the drifting smoke, but he couldn't help himself, and stared into one of the bee's bulbous, black eyes. At first all he could see was his own reflection in the shiny surface, but then he saw something else he couldn't explain. There was sadness in those eyes, and Tom felt it as if it were his own.

"Tom?" Randolf asked. "What is it?"

Tom looked away, and the emotion faded. "Nothing," he said quickly, glancing over his shoulder at the sentries. "It's nothing."

"Good," Randolf said. "The bears and the Rats have sped up, and so must we if we don't want to lose them."

Tom quickened his pace, helping the warrior priest to pull the empty cart, but he couldn't completely shake that strange, sad sensation. He sensed that it had something to do with his reason for being there.

The stone corridor dipped downward, sending them deeper into the caverns beneath the mountain. They passed many worker bees as they descended, but the smoke that continued to drift through the cave took away any interest the bees might have had in the strangers. The Rat Creatures and the bears were moving quickly, the bear brothers whispering excitedly as they got closer to the hive — and the honey.

The rock corridor suddenly dropped precipitately, and ahead of them smoke had collected, appearing almost like a wall before them. But the bears and the Rats didn't slow down one bit, plunging into the undulating cloud of gray.

Tom and Randolf hesitated, listening for sounds of commotion, but heard nothing other than excited chatter.

"I guess it's safe," Randolf said, and the pair continued on into the shifting curtain of smoke, pulling the cart behind them.

Tom coughed and tried to wave away the noxious fumes with his hand. He could still hear the others, but he could also hear something else.

He stopped walking and released his grip on the wagon. He started to address Randolf but found himself speechless in the smoky mist. He reached out, fumbling to find the priest.

"Randolf?" he managed to choke out.

Tom stumbled forward, emerging into another corridor with far less smoke. He looked through watering eyes for his companions but saw no one. Standing in the stone passage, he closed his eyes and listened, hoping to hear the voices of the bears, but he heard something else instead.

The sound was like a small voice calling to him, though not with words. It was like a sad song, coming from somewhere down this new corridor.

He had no choice but to go to it.

"Uncle Percy says the smoker is burning up fuel faster than he thought," Abbey said. "We're gonna need a lot more stuff from the woods."

Abbey, Barclay, and Roderick were hunched over, scanning the forest floor for more moss, twigs, and dried leaves.

"This looks pretty good," Roderick said, loading some tree remnants into his arms. "They're really dry, so they should smoke nicely."

"We've got to move fast," the little girl Bone reminded them. "Nothing to burn means no smoke, and no smoke means . . ."

"That somebody's gonna get stung good," Barclay said, heading farther down the mountainside.

"Don't go too far, Barclay!" Abbey called out.

"Yeah, yeah, yeah," her twin replied, annoyed by his

sister's pestering. "I think there's some of that moss stuff down here, and Uncle Percy says that burns the best."

Abbey was suddenly interested. "Where?" she asked, following her brother.

"Don't you worry about where," Barclay answered, speeding up.

"Hey, guys!" Roderick called out, his arms full of sticks. "There's plenty of stuff right here!"

But Abbey wasn't listening. She wanted to find the moss, and wasn't about to let her brother get to it first. She went too fast and stumbled, landing on her butt, and began to slide.

"Whooaaa!" she cried out.

Hearing her, Barclay started to turn. "Abbey, you stupid —" he began as she collided with him, their heads knocking together with an audible *clunk*.

And then they were tumbling, squealing, shrieking, and grunting, rolling down the side of the mountain. They finally came to a painful stop against an old broken tree stump.

"Ohhhhhhhh, my head," Barclay moaned.

"You and your bright ideas," Abbey said, plucking leaves from the front of her dress. "If you'd just stayed put, we wouldn't have almost got ourselves killed."

Roderick ran down the slope toward them, careful not

to slide like his friends did. "Are you two all right?" he cried.

"I'm fine," Barclay said, standing carefully. "No thanks to my stupid sister."

"What're you blaming me for," Abbey retorted, brushing dirt from her butt. "If you'd-a listened . . ."

Barclay suddenly tilted his head to one side. "Listen," he said.

"Yeah, if you'd-a listened to me —" Abbey went on.

"No, listen," Barclay corrected.

"Are those voices?" Roderick asked.

Abbey was paying attention now. "Voices? Who else could be way out here?" she wondered aloud.

"Shhhhh," Barclay said, putting a finger to his mouth as he peeked through some thick underbrush into the forest below them.

"What do you see?" Abbey asked, moving to a spot close beside him.

Multiple Rat Creatures emerged from the deep, dark forest. Their faces were close to the ground, sniffing as if on the trail of something.

Barclay gulped, and Abbey gasped.

"I want to see, too," Roderick said, trying to wriggle between the twins. "Oh my gosh!" he said as he lost his footing and slid down the hill in an avalanche of rocks and dirt.

Barclay reached out to grab Roderick by the scruff of his neck, but it was too late. The commotion had already caught the attention of the Rats.

"Hssssssssssssssssssssssssssssssssssssss," the Rats hissed, raising their noses and looking upward, the Constable and his men close by.

"We've gotta get out of here and warn Uncle Percy!" Abbey said, and then took off running back up the hill.

"I saw them first, so I get to tell him!" Barclay cried out, scrambling right behind her.

"Don't you two ever stop?" Roderick asked, following the twins as they raced to find their uncle.

"What was that?" one of the Rat soldiers asked his brethren as he peered up the hill.

Another Rat sniffed at the air. "I'm not sure," he growled.

King Agak bounded over to them. "What is it?" the King asked.

"Something was moving," one of them said.

"And we smelled something," said the other. "But now it is gone."

Agak snarled, moving closer to the base of the mountain. He tilted his head back, taking a great lungful of the forest air into his hairy chest. And then, slowly, a smile grew on his monstrous features.

"What is it?" the Constable asked, moving closer.

"I know that smell." The King looked back up the hill.

"Bones," he said, licking his chops. "The delicious smell of Bones."

Percival peered down into the hole, watching as the thick haze from the smoker wafted into the darkness.

It was killing him to be here, just standing by, doing nothing. He was an explorer, after all, and there wasn't anything he wanted to do more than explore. Looking down into the opening, Percival imagined what might wait below: sights never before seen by any Bone. He imagined speaking to the stuffed shirts at the Boneville Explorers' Society, describing the spectacular things he'd seen on his journey to the Valley.

Percival didn't need a mirror to know that he was grinning like an idiot. What a night that would be, finally getting the attention that he deserved.

But the thrill of exploration quickly evaporated as he reminded himself that he was going nowhere near the inside of that cave system. He was needed here. And besides, he had no interest in wearing a bee costume, thank you very much.

He turned his attention back to the smoker, reaching out to open the door to its belly. He sure hoped the kids returned soon with some more fuel, because the device was nearly empty. A small pile of twigs and dried moss was all that remained, and Percival was just about to feed it to the smoker, when he heard the cries.

"Uncle Percy!" Abbey shrieked.

Percival stepped away from the smoker, careful not to lose his footing on the slippery slope of the mountainside.

Abbey was climbing toward him as fast as she could, Barclay right behind her, and Roderick farther back, straining on all fours to catch up.

"What's all the commotion about?" Percival asked as he reached down to help the twins.

Abbey was breathing too hard to answer.

"We've got trouble," Barclay managed to gasp.

Abbey punched him in the stomach before he could say any more. "I told you I was telling him. The Rat Creatures and the Constable are coming!" she exclaimed, pointing down into the woods below.

Squinting, Percival followed her direction and found it — a trail of Rat Creatures heading their way.

"Not good," Percival said, a knot the size of a football forming in his stomach. "Not good at all."

A more persistent flow of air was blowing through the tunnels now, and Randolf found himself growing anxious. The smoke was gradually dissipating.

He turned toward Tom, and his anxiety heightened

when he realized that the boy was no longer beside him.

"Tom?" Randolf called out, eyes darting around the darkened passage. Panic was setting in, but he managed to wrestle control from his fears. The boy had probably just gone off on his own in search of the Spark. *He'll be fine*, the Veni Yan told himself. *After all, he is our leader.*

No matter how many times he told himself this, he still couldn't quite bring himself to believe it. But the Dreaming often worked in mysterious ways, and if he and Tom were to be separated for this leg of the journey, then maybe there was a reason.

Randolf struggled with the idea of going in search of the boy, but heard the bears cry out up ahead. Struggling with the cart, Randolf carried on through the wafting smoke and into a cavernous chamber.

The Rats and the bears were furiously moving about. Randolf dropped the cart, drew his sword from beneath his bee costume, and moved to join them.

"What is it?" he asked. "Why did you cry out?"

"We've done it!" Bobby said, dark eyes wide and twinkling with excitement. "We've made it inside the honeycomb."

The air had cleared enough to show Randolf that they had indeed found their way into the bees' honey chamber. The cavern was huge, the walls covered in large, six-sided cells made from beeswax. Giant bees were everywhere, but they didn't really seem to notice the intruders. Even still,

Randolf remained uneasy, especially since the air appeared to be clearing.

"I suggest we move quickly," he said, eyeing the bees, but Bobby wasn't listening. Instead he ran over to where Al and Joey had already broken into one of the combs and all three began to sample the golden liquid inside.

"They really seem to like that," Stinky said to Smelly as they watched the bears.

"I wonder if we would?" mused Smelly.

"I doubt it," Stinky replied. "If it doesn't scream when you bite into it, where's the thrill?"

"So true," Smelly agreed.

Randolf didn't have time for this. There was less and less smoke in the chamber and he thought he saw signs of the bees becoming more alert. He glanced toward the entrance, fighting the urge to go off in search of Tom. A loud cracking sound distracted him, and he looked over to see that the bears were now breaking away huge pieces of the honey-filled combs.

"What are you doing?" Randolf asked.

"Never mind the questions," Joey said. "Bring the cart over here and help us."

Randolf watched as the bears continued to remove large chunks of the wall and stack them on the floor. "Is that wise?" he asked, looking from the bears to the real bees, and back again.

"How else are we going to get the honey back home?" Al asked, breaking away another huge portion of honeycomb with a grunt.

Randolf didn't like it one bit, but he retrieved the cart anyway, dragged it across the room, and set it in front of the bears.

"They seem very good at this," Smelly said as he watched the bears tear the honeycombs from the wall.

"Those are three bears that really love their work," Stinky offered.

Randolf began loading stacks of honeycombs onto the cart. "Don't you think this is enough?" he finally asked them.

"Are the walls bare yet?" Bobby asked, ripping away a huge, dripping hunk of comb and placing it in the cart. "If they're not, then we aren't done."

Joey and Al added more comb to the growing stack, the excitement keeping the normally sleepy bear awake.

"Listen to me," the Veni Yan said. "This is exactly what I was afraid would happen. You're letting your greed get away from you."

"This has nothing to do with greed," Bobby said as he loaded more pieces onto the cart. "We've been working for this for years — this is payment for our hard work and suffering."

"I've dreamed of this," Joey said, moving to start tearing apart another section of wall.

"Every time I fall asleep, I see this," Al said, helping his brother. "That's a lot of dreaming about honey."

Randolf looked around the honeycomb chamber and saw that the smoke was finally all gone, and the air was clean and fresh. And the bees that were once so docile? They were gradually waking up and would not be happy with what they saw. Randolf thought they still had some time, though. If they could *slowly* leave the chamber, they just might be able to . . .

An alarm bell was suddenly ringing, filling the chamber with its jarring sound, and they all looked over to see Al standing there, the strange device around his neck ringing away.

"See, it works," the Bear said proudly, and then turned off the alarm.

The bear was right, it had awakened him.

But it had also snapped the bees to attention, riling them to attack.

CHAPTER 15

"I had hoped you would come," the Nacht said, swimming around Lorimar in the darkness. She was paralyzed by his presence, the raw power emanating from this dark being rendering her silent.

"Do I frighten you?" he asked. "If so, I apologize, for that is not my intention."

The Dragon circled her and the sphere that contained the untainted piece of the Dreaming.

"And what is your intention?" she asked, finding her voice and trying to be brave.

"To bring you here," the Nacht answered. "To show you this." The Dragon of darkness stopped, looming above the sphere, and peered down at the world inside. "I've saved it for you," the great beast said.

Lorimar was shocked by the Dragon's words. "For me?" she asked. "Why would you . . . ?"

"Does it not bring you joy to see this?" the Nacht asked. "Does it not make you happy to see that you are not alone?"

She was drawn to the bubble again, peering at a piece of something she'd long thought destroyed. From out of the green they came, members of her race emerging from their hiding places.

"How?" she asked, more to her people than to the beast that loomed above her.

"They were lost between worlds," the Nacht explained. "Trapped in a place neither here nor there . . . Ghost Circles, I believe they're called."

The Dragon unfurled his impressive wingspan, and then closed it around himself and the sphere.

Lorimar gasped.

"I rescued them," said the Nacht. "I gave them a place where they could live out their lives." He paused, turning his mighty head to look at her with his burning eyes. "Where you could live out your existence, away from all the hardship and darkness that is coming . . . and you do know that it's coming."

"Yes," Lorimar answered softly.

"This could be yours, Lorimar," the Nacht purred, allowing her a glimpse of the sphere again.

It had been so long since she'd actually been happy. Here was her chance to regain everything she had lost. But at what price?

"How?" she asked, refusing to look at him. The fact that she had asked the question filled her with shame.

"The Spark," the Nacht said. "Once it is gathered . . . once it is made whole . . ."

She looked up at him then, sucked into the fire of his eyes, and she knew then and there.

"You will bring it to me."

Lorimar knew that she was doomed.

Tom followed the sad, strange sound. Down a winding passage he walked until he reached an opening into a much larger area. Inside were two worker bees, but they were still under the effects of the smoke and didn't pay him any mind.

An eerie yellow glow seemed to come from the six-sided chambers that covered the walls, illuminating the vast space. The strange siren call was loudest here. Tom walked farther into the room, no longer hearing just one voice, but many joined together.

A sudden warmth against his chest made him glance down and he saw the glow from beneath his costume. He pulled out the necklace, the stone pulsing with a powerful inner light.

Tom held the Spark in one hand and walked about the room, studying the many compartments as he went, until he noticed one particular chamber. It was high up on the wall and glowed stronger and brighter than all the others, the closer he got to it.

He stood beneath the chamber, the beat of life from the Spark in his hand matching the pulse of the inner glow from the chamber above.

Tom grabbed hold of the rough edges of the six-sided combs and began to climb. He reached the special comb, the light behind its thin, waxen covering throbbing with life. Holding tightly to the outer wall with one hand, he carefully pulled away the soft wax with the other, gaining him access.

The light from inside the comb nearly blinded him, and the humming in his head was all he could hear. But none of that stopped him. Tom reached inside the comb, fingers brushing against the hard, crystalline shape that nested there, and snatched it up.

He withdrew his hand and gazed at the newest piece of Spark that glowed in his fingers.

The sliver then seemed to come to life, jumping from his hand to meld with the fragment of Spark around his neck. Tom gasped as the pieces joined, and the power of this new addition passed through him. The feeling was so intense, he thought he might burst.

Tom knew he was falling, but he could do nothing to stop it. He landed on his back, looking up at the multitude of six-sided compartments.

Suddenly, he could see inside each and every one of them: the beauty, and the sorrow, of what was contained within.

No wonder the song is so sad, Tom thought.

He wasn't sure how long he'd been lying on the floor of the chamber when he began to hear a commotion. Slowly he got to his feet, his back sore, but nothing he couldn't handle. He checked the Spark hanging around his neck and saw that it glowed softly, as if content to have another one of its sisters back. He tucked it inside his bee costume and prepared to leave.

The bees of the hive were still buzzing, but now it didn't sound at all peaceful. It sounded angry . . . and then it dawned on him.

The smoke was gone.

Tom raced for the chamber entrance, only to find his way blocked by two worker bees — fully awake and none too happy with the intruder.

"Okay now," Tom said, raising his hands. "I know I shouldn't be in here but —"

The sound of voices outside the chamber interrupted him, and Tom looked past the advancing worker bees to see the bear brothers, the Rats, and Randolf hurrying by, pulling the cart laden with what looked to be pieces of the honeycomb wall.

"Hey!" Tom cried out.

The bees were stalking closer now, and he could feel the wall of the hive at his back.

"There you are," Randolf Clearmeadow said, brandishing his sword as he strode into the chamber. The bears and the Rats followed, dragging the cart behind them.

The bees began to furiously flap their wings, lifting their bodies into the air as they prepared to attack.

"Wait!" Tom cried out. He ran over to join his friends as the bees hovered angrily, bending their bodies forward to reveal their stingers.

"Get behind me, Tom," the Veni Yan priest instructed.

"I'll deal with these monsters —"

"No," Tom shouted. "You're not going to fight them, and we're not going to run." He reached out and touched Randolf's hand, pushing down the sword.

And then he walked toward the angry bees.

More bees flew into the chamber, filling the air with an intense hum. It was as his vision had shown him: the sounds of the bees, the sight of their giant, yellow and black forms, their anger as they realized they were being invaded.

"Tom, don't . . ." Randolf called out.

But Tom ignored the priest, stopping only when he was almost directly beneath the hovering insects. Since he was the only one moving, the insects saw him as the deadliest threat. A swarm of soldier bees circled him, readying their stingers.

Tom was surprised that he wasn't more afraid. He reached beneath his costume to again grab hold of the still warm and pulsing fragment of Spark, as the giant insects struck.

The boy is a fool was all Randolf could think as he watched Tom attract the solider bees' attention.

He wanted to go to his aid, but there was something in the boy's voice, something that compelled him to stay where he was.

Confidence? Randolf had no idea, but whatever it was, he knew that it would do little good once those monsters attacked.

The tension was thick in the stagnant air of the hive, and Randolf watched in horror as the bees came down, their long, pointed stingers aimed at their prey.

"No!" Randolf screamed, leaping into action. But there came a tremendous burst of light, and the Veni Yan was driven back, nearly blinded from the intensity of the glow. As he blinked away shapes of dancing black that moved across his line of sight, he expected to see Tom lying on the ground, stung and dying, or possibly even already dead.

He never expected what he actually saw. The bees were gathered around him. Tom stood in the center of the large, furry mass of humming insects, the Spark in hand and raised above his head.

"We mean you no harm," Randolf heard Tom say to the giant bugs, and Randolf knew that they understood him. "I need to see your Queen at once," Tom added. "I have something very important to tell her."

That was when Randolf finally understood: Despite the fact that Tom was just a boy, he was indeed something special. And if need be, Randolf Clearmeadow had no doubt that he would follow him to the ends of the earth.

Percival moved as fast as he could down the side of the mountain toward the woods below, but it was still slow going. The slope was treacherous and he had to check each step carefully before motioning for the kids to follow.

"C'mon, c'mon," he said impatiently, reaching up to give Abbey a hand.

"But what about the smoker?" she asked, ignoring his hand and scrambling down beside him.

"There's no choice but to abandon it," the adventurer said. He scanned the hill from where they'd come, looking for the Rats and the possessed lawmen's bodies. "Besides, it was pretty much out of smoke anyway."

"But what about the bees?" Roderick asked.

"Yeah," Barclay echoed. "Won't the bees wake up without the smoke?"

"Yep, they probably will," Percival agreed, his eyes on the woods ahead.

"So what about Tom and Randolf, and the bears, and those two stinky Rats?" Abbey asked, pausing on a rock.

Percival stopped and turned to look at her as Roderick and Barclay stumbled past. "Don't worry about them," he said. He moved back up the hill a bit and took the little Bone's hand. "They've already had plenty of time to carry out their part of the mission." He led her down the slope, following her brother and the raccoon.

A buzzing filled the air then, and suddenly the explorer wasn't so sure about his friends' success.

"It's getting loud," Abbey commented. She stopped and placed a hand to her brow as she looked up at the sky. "And they sound kinda mad."

"Nah," Percival said as he gave her hand a tug. "That's just how bees sound."

He would never have admitted that his niece might be right, but there was a certain intensity to the buzzing and that made him a little nervous. He rushed Abbey toward Roderick and Barclay, who were now waiting for them at the bottom of the mountain.

The buzzing was closer now — and Percival chanced a quick look up and over his shoulder. The sky was filled with a swarm, and there was no hiding the fact that they were indeed angry. He tried not to think about why that would be — perhaps because a gang of humans, bears, and Rats had invaded their hive?

He and Abbey had reached the other two, when Barclay pointed behind his uncle. "Look!" he cried.

Percival didn't want to turn around, but he did, and got an eyeful.

The Rats, shaggy faces pressed to the ground, were just coming over the top of the mountainside. They were moving fast, and the Bone figured it wouldn't be long before they caught up to his little group.

"Into the woods," Percival ordered, waving his arms to herd the kids ahead.

"What are we gonna do, Uncle Percy?" Barclay asked in a shaky voice as they entered the forest.

"I don't know yet," he said. "I'm thinking."

They kept running.

"Anything yet?" Roderick asked after a few minutes.

"Still thinking," Percival answered, panting. He glanced up through the trees to see bees swarming the skies, searching for an enemy to attack. And the nugget of a crazy idea began to form.

"Well?" Abbey asked.

Percival checked behind them and saw movement in the woods. The Rats were close.

"Uncle Percy, I'm getting tired," Barclay whined.

"Hang in there, kid," Percival encouraged. Ahead he could see a small clearing. "Head over there," he told the kids, pointing to the break in the trees.

"What are we doing?" Barclay asked.

"Do you have a plan?" Roderick wanted to know.

"Of course he has a plan," Abbey answered.

"Okay, stop here," Percival ordered, bending over to catch his breath. They were at the edge of the clearing, the Rats not too far behind them.

"Okay, here's what we're gonna do," the adventurer began. The kids gathered around him, listening intently.

"See those bees?" He pointed to the sky, and the kids nodded. "We want to get their attention," he said.

As one, Abbey, Barclay, and Roderick looked at him, eyes wide, believing that at that moment, Uncle Percy had finally lost all his marbles.

"But that means they'll see us . . ." Barclay began.

"And come down here and . . ." Abbey continued.

"Exactly," Percival said, without letting either of them finish. The twins looked terrified, but Roderick, who had been watching the impending arrival of the Nacht's servants, turned his gaze to the bee-filled sky. A sly smile appeared on his hairy raccoon face.

"You're a genius," he said.

"I try," Percival replied, happy that at least one of them understood. "Now," the Bone adventurer said, rubbing his hands together. "Let's make some noise."

It won't be long now, the Constable thought with a widening grin as he and his deputies followed King Agak and the Rat Creatures through the trees.

He imagined how grateful Lord Nacht would be when told of their victory, hoping this human body would be his reward.

A noise from somewhere ahead of them interrupted his thoughts, and he stopped to listen.

"What is that sound?" King Agak asked.

"Birds?" one of the deputies suggested.

"Maybe it's the wind?" offered another.

The third shook his head. "It's screaming," he said with finality.

"Screaming?" questioned the Rat King.

"Screaming," the Constable repeated, his smile return-ing from beneath his thick mustache. "Our enemies know their fates are sealed." He rubbed his hands together in anticipation of the horrors to come.

"They're screaming because they're afraid?" asked one of the Rat soldiers.

"Precisely," the Constable said.

"Well, what are we waiting for?" Agak asked, his slimy tongue protruding eagerly from his mouth.

"Let's go, then!" the Constable proclaimed, and Rats and possessed humans alike charged forward, eager to find their frightened quarry huddling in fear.

They rushed through the forest. Nothing could stop them — nothing could slow them down. This was the mo-ment they'd all been waiting for. The cries grew louder now, making them move all the faster. The Constable could not wait to see their frightened faces as he and the others sprang from a thicket of saplings with murder in their twisted hearts.

Yes, there was terror on their faces, and they were screaming at the top of their lungs, but the three Bones and the raccoon were running toward the Constable and his men and the Rats, a swarm of angry bees right behind them, skimming above the forest floor in hot pursuit.

Correction. A swarm of *giant* angry bees.

"Wait," the Constable ordered, holding out his hands,

but the Bones and raccoon dove beneath his legs and into the underbrush.

"What just happened?" King Agak asked, looking around for his prey.

The Constable didn't reply. Instead his eyes were locked on the swarm of yellow and black insects that were flying at them.

Their nasty-looking stingers were poised to strike, and it didn't take a genius to know that they were going to hurt.

At first they tried to fight, but their swords, fangs, and claws proved to be futile against the fury of the bees. They had no choice but to flee. Even as they ran, they were attacked, stingers painfully poking their tender human flesh.

Maybe having a human body isn't the best idea, after all, the Constable thought as he ran crazily through the woods with his deputies and the Rat Creatures.

The sound of buzzing mixed with yelps and screams was like a strange kind of music to Percival's ears.

"Keep running!" he shouted to the twins and Roderick ahead of him. He didn't know how much time the bees would buy them.

Abbey tripped and stumbled, but Barclay was there to help her up, holding on to her hand as they both continued to run.

Maybe there is hope for them, Percival thought, smiling,

until he saw Abbey pull her hand away and playfully slap the back of her brother's head. She raced ahead of him, laughing hysterically.

Roderick, meanwhile, had disappeared into some thick brush. Percival was about to holler for him when the young raccoon reappeared.

"Hey, in here!" he cried, jumping up and down excitedly. "Wait till you see what I found!"

The twins raced to see who would be the first to see Roderick's discovery, while Percival quickly followed.

"What've you got?" the Bone explorer asked, pushing through the thick bushes. "Well, I'll be," he said, emerging from the woods to find himself standing before a large entrance to another cave in the base of the mountain.

"This'll be a good place to hide until the Rats and the bees are gone," Roderick said, doing a little dance.

"That's a good idea," Percival said. He cocked his head to one side, listening to the sounds of the woods, not hearing anything other than the chirps and squawks of forest life. "Let's get out of sight." He began herding the kids toward the opening.

Barclay and Roderick had already disappeared into the darkness of the cave. "C'mon, guys!" the little Bone called out, his voice fading into the passage.

"Wait for us!" Percival called out, grabbing Abbey's hand.

"Yeah, wait up, you big dummy!" Abbey yelled.

The entrance opened into a long, winding passage that seemed to go deep into the mountain. After several minutes of traveling in the dark, Percival ordered them all to stop.

"This should be far enough," he said. It was so dark now, he wasn't sure where anyone else was standing. "We'll just sit tight here for a bit."

"It's awfully dark in here," he heard Abbey say, the tone of her voice telling him that she was afraid.

"What's the matter, Abs?" Barclay taunted. "Are ya scared?"

"That'll be enough of that," Percival admonished. "Why don't you guys make yourself useful and feel around for some twigs to start a small fire?"

He heard them scrabble around in the dark as he fished in one of the many pockets of his shirt for a match.

"Here ya go, Uncle Percy," Roderick said from nearby.

The Bone squatted and ran his hand over the floor of the cave until he found the small pile of sticks. "This should be good," he said as he lit the match and placed it against the twigs, breathing a sigh of relief as flickering light filled the chamber.

"That's what I'm talking about," he said cheerfully, gazing into the flames.

"Uh, Uncle Percy," Barclay said. "Maybe that's not such a great idea."

"Now, why wouldn't it be?" the explorer asked as he turned toward his nephew — and froze.

Giant bees were clogging the passage, fluttering their wings menacingly.

Percival motioned for the kids to come closer, and they huddled together as the bees marched toward them.

"What are we gonna do, Uncle Percy?" Barclay asked in a frightened whisper.

Percival's adventurer's mind was already working over-time. He was going to suggest they run, but he doubted they would get very far. "Don't you worry about a thing," he said instead. He left the kids and walked toward the closest of the bees.

The giant insect reared back with a scary buzz that sounded like a runaway chain saw. Percival looked the big insect firmly in its large, black eyes and cleared his throat.

"Take me to your leader," he said, hoping the bee would understand. He wasn't sure if it did, but the swarm quickly surrounded them. All he could do was hope for the best.

Chapter 16

The bees had understood Tom's request and were leading them to their Queen.

He had warned them all to be on their best behavior, stressing this point to the bears in particular. Fearing the sting of the giant bees, the three bears had wanted to try and flee the hive with their stolen honey, but Tom had managed to convince them that this wouldn't be wise, and to trust him.

They were ushered down a long rock corridor, the giant bees moving them along until they reached a large arch of rock that opened into an even larger chamber.

An egg chamber, to be precise.

Entering the room, Tom saw that it was similar to the chamber he'd been in earlier, but this one was much bigger.

"Is this another honey room?" Al asked excitedly.

"Egg chamber," Tom corrected.

"I enjoy eggs more than honey," he heard Smelly whisper.

"I wonder if they have a bacon chamber?" Stinky asked his partner.

Tom was about to explain to them that it was a bee egg chamber, where the new bees of the hive were born, but he didn't get the chance. Two of the larger bees, special sentries to the hive, he imagined, came at him. They singled him from the others and moved him toward another part of the chamber. Tom saw that Randolf was distressed by this.

"It's all right," Tom assured him as he allowed the two giant insects to escort him.

At an opening in the chamber wall, the two escorts blocked his path, allowing him no farther. Tom waited, his eyes scanning the room and the six-sided egg compartments that covered the walls. The Spark pulsed around his neck, and he sensed what was happening in this egg chamber, as well as all the others spread throughout the vast mountain hive.

This was what he needed to speak to the Queen about, and he hoped that she would listen.

The Queen Bee emerged from the passage, larger and much longer in body type than any of the other bees that they had encountered since entering the hive. With the way that she moved, Tom could sense that she was troubled.

And he knew why.

The sentry bees moved away, exposing him to the waiting Queen. He could feel the intensity of her gaze, and Tom knew that she wasn't in the mood to deal with intruders.

"My Queen," Tom began, bowing his head and dropping to one knee. "First I must apologize, for myself, and for my friends," he continued. "We had no right to invade your home and take your honey, but we were looking for something inside your hive that is very important to our mission . . . a quest we are undertaking." Tom reached into his costume and produced the piece of the Spark.

The Queen fluttered her wings, buzzing in response to his words. Tom found that he could understand her language, and again marveled at the power of the Spark.

She wanted to know about the object found in her hive, and of the quest. He attempted to explain.

"I was looking for a piece to add to this," Tom said, holding up the Spark to the Queen. It throbbed with a warm, yellow light before her, and Tom believed that it was somehow communicating with the insect leader. "Another piece to help restore the first spark of light that drove back the darkness at the beginning of time."

The Queen hummed and buzzed, hard mandibles inside her mouth clicking noisily. She wanted to know if he had found what he was looking for.

"Yes, I did," Tom answered her. "And when it joined

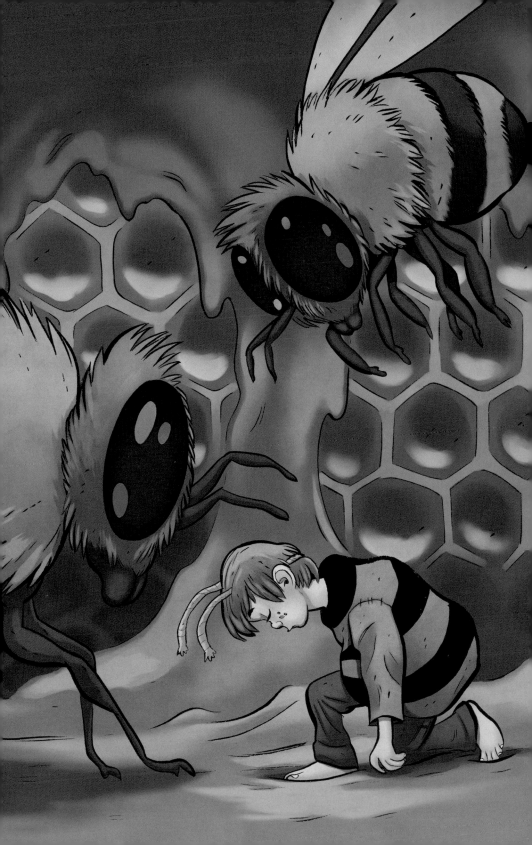

the piece I already have, it told me of your troubles." Tom looked around the chamber. "It told me about your babies."

Tom had no understanding of what he had been hearing when he'd entered the first of the egg chambers, but when the latest shard of the Spark had been joined with the others, it all became painfully clear to him.

The unborn bees of the hive, in their sealed, six-sided chambers, were being touched by the evil of the Nacht. Their development into full-grown bees was stunted by the influence of the nightmare creature that had infected the Dreaming.

Tom looked back to the Queen.

"I know that something is hurting your babies," he told her. "And it is *that* something that my friends and I are trying to stop."

The Queen wanted to know about the evil.

"It is called the Nacht," Tom explained. "He is reaching out through the darkness — through the Dreaming — to the Waking World."

The Queen hummed her next question to him, desperate to know why this Nacht would want to harm her hive . . . her children.

"I don't really know," he said truthfully. "I think he's just bad . . . and wants to see the Valley, and the whole world, changed to be that way, too."

The Queen was quiet for some time. He knew she was

thinking about the threat to her hive, and its future.

"Let us be on our way, and I promise that my friends and I will do everything we can to stop the Nacht," he told her in all earnestness.

The Queen and Tom looked into each other's eyes, a connection forming between human and insect, two very different species threatened by the same danger.

Tom sensed that she was about to answer, when there was a commotion from the back of the egg chamber.

He turned and half expected to see the bears acting up, but instead saw that there were new players causing a scene. Through the archway of the Queen's chamber marched several bees along with three Bones and a raccoon.

"I'm going, I'm going!" the Bone adventurer barked at one of the more aggressive worker bees. "Stop your pushing."

"Percival," Tom cried, climbing to his feet, glad to see him and the kids. He had worried that the dwindling smoke meant something grim had happened to his friends.

"Tom!" Abbey cried, running to throw her arms around him. "I'm so glad you didn't get stung to death."

"Uh, yeah," Tom said, a little embarrassed by her show of affection.

"We woulda kept making the smoke, but we got chased off-a the mountain by the Constable and his men, and the Rats," Barclay explained.

"But we showed them," Roderick said. "Led the bees right to 'em."

Tom looked at Percival. "The Constable?" he asked.

Percival nodded. "Yeah, he and the Rats must've been following our trail. We managed to get away, but then we got picked up by some pretty angry bees."

"They're angry that we've invaded their hive," Tom said, "but I've just explained about our quest."

The bees in the egg chamber were growing in number and they circled, emitting a low, menacing hum.

"How was that working out?" Percival asked, looking around nervously.

"I told you we should have run when we had the chance," Bobby said.

Tom moved closer to his friends and they all stood together as the bees converged.

"It appears your words of impending danger did little to convince them," Randolf observed.

"But I thought she understood," Tom said, unsure of what they should do next. "We were going to help save the hive." He tensed as the bees flew closer and closer still, their stingers emerging.

And just as he was about to give up hope, the bees withdrew.

"Something's happening," Randolf said. Tom noticed that the warrior priest was clutching his sword tightly in his hand, not intent to go down without a fight.

Bobby, who had closed his eyes, opened one and looked around. "Why aren't we stung?" he asked. His brothers were just as surprised.

The worker bees had flown across the chamber to amass by their Queen. Tom could see that she was fluttering her wings and releasing a sound: It told her soldiers that the strangers were not to be harmed.

"Whatever just happened, I'm all for it," Percival said as he hugged the twins closer.

Tom walked toward the Queen and again bowed his head. "Thank you," he said.

The Queen buzzed in response, her movements strangely dancelike as she fluttered her wings and moved around in a circle.

Tom bowed once more and returned to his friends. "We can go now," he said, leading them toward the entrance.

"What about the Nacht's people?" Percival asked. "They might still be waiting out there."

"The Queen said her soldiers are dealing with them," Tom answered. "We should be safe for now."

"What else did she say, Tom?" Abbey wanted to know.

"She asked us to save her hive," he said as they left the egg chamber. "And I told her that we would . . . or die trying."

· · ·

The evil spirit wearing the body of the Constable loved everything about his physical experience, except the pain. It was dark now, and it appeared that they had managed to outrun the yellow and black monsters, but not before feeling the fury of their stingers many times.

His body throbbed from multiple stings, and from the looks of things, his brothers — as well as the Rats — weren't doing much better. They had found shelter beneath the roots of a gnarled and twisted old tree, burrowing down into the cold damp earth to hide and heal their wounds.

The Rat King and his soldiers continued to grumble about their hunger, furious that they did not yet have the meat of Bones in their bellies, going silent only when they'd fallen asleep from exhaustion.

Huddled there in the darkness, the Constable could feel the accusing eyes of his brothers upon him. They did not care to be stung, and disliked even more the painful welts that covered their bodies.

But the evil spirit experienced an even deeper pain than that caused by the venom of giant insects. He experienced the pain of failure — a hurt that traveled to the core of his being.

The champions of the Dreaming had thwarted them again.

It made the borrowed heart within his chest heavy

with grief. He had failed his brothers . . . the Rats . . . and his master.

The Nacht.

It was with the thought of his dark lord that the Constable's world began to spin, and he found himself no longer sharing a hole beneath the roots of a giant tree, but someplace else entirely. Someplace familiar, but one that he had not seen since embarking on the mission to destroy the Dreaming's champions.

Plucked from his human body, the evil spirit floated naked and exposed in a place that he'd once called home. Suddenly, he was in the presence of the one he knew as his master.

"You've failed me . . . again," the Nacht said in a voice that seemed to come from everywhere.

The spirit's first instinct was to flee, but the Nacht was indeed everywhere. There was no place to hide.

"I-I'm sorry, m-my lord," the spirit stammered nervously. "The Dreaming's champions are proving far more elusive than we expected. Even with the help of the Rat King and his soldiers, the chosen boy, Tom Elm, has managed to evade our efforts."

"No matter," the Nacht said.

The spirit fearfully continued with his excuses. "But don't you worry about us, dark sir, oh no, we've got a plan to — Did you just say 'no matter'?"

"Yes," the Nacht growled. "It is no matter, for I have already set in motion the means by which these champions will be brought down."

"You . . . you have?" the spirit questioned.

The shadow Dragon nodded its massive head, a jagged smile forming.

"I have," the Nacht said.

"If I could be so bold . . . How?" the spirit asked curiously.

"Within their very midst I have planted the seed of their doom," the Dragon said, amused by his own words.

One of his powerful clawed feet rose in the darkness, his taloned fingers splaying apart to display something very tiny in his palm. The spirit floated closer, his curiosity canceling out his fear.

In the Dragon's palm rested a tiny acorn.

"I . . . I don't understand, my lord."

"From within," the Nacht said, closing his claws around the tiny seed. "They will be destroyed from within."

Chapter 17

Tom was standing in the forest, with the bears and all of his friends, staring up into the trees at the *Queen of the Sky*.

"That's a problem," Percival said, rubbing his chin in thought.

"A real predicament," Bobby agreed.

"Maybe if we . . ." Joey said, gazing up into the trees. "Naw, that wouldn't work." The bear went back to thinking.

"I've got it!" said Al excitedly, but then he fell asleep and promptly woke up again as the alarm clock chimed. "What was I saying?" he asked, dazed.

The two Rats were huddled off to themselves, and Tom could hear them talking.

"Why can't we just fly the craft from the trees?" asked Stinky as he petted his dead squirrel affectionately.

"Because the balloons are punctured," Smelly said with more intelligence than Tom expected. "And in order to repair them, the ship must be brought down to the ground."

"And how do they intend to do that?" Stinky asked.

"That is the problem we are facing," Smelly replied.

"Great," Stinky responded with a roll of his bulbous eyes. "Agak will have his claws on us, and my beloved Fredrick, for sure."

Abbey approached Percival and slipped her tiny hand into his.

"How are we gonna get the *Queen* down, Uncle Percy?" she asked.

"Don't really know just yet," the Bone adventurer said. He released her hand and paced the forest floor beneath the ship.

"But you'll come up with an answer soon, right?" Barclay asked him.

Percival didn't say anything, and that made Tom more nervous. Time was of the essence. The Nacht's power was growing, his evil spreading across the Valley at an increasing rate. They had to leave the forest and continue their quest before . . .

"We may need to leave on foot."

Tom looked to see Randolf standing beside him.

"I was thinking the same thing," Tom said solemnly.

"Of course you were," Randolf said, looking to him. "It's how a leader would think."

There was something different about the warrior priest,

Tom thought, something that had happened since the hive. An attitude change. Tom didn't know what had happened, exactly, but he liked that Randolf now seemed more willing to trust him.

"The *Queen* needs to stay where she is if we have any intentions of stopping the Nacht," Tom said. They didn't have the time to wait around for somebody to come up with a way to bring the *Queen* down to the ground for repairs.

"Though I'm not sure if Percival will want to leave his ship," Tom said, staring up at the sky ship perched in the trees.

"It is his choice to come with us or stay behind," Randolf said coldly. "The quest waits for no one."

Tom nodded. "You're right," he said. "I'll go talk to him."

"And I'll gather some supplies for our journey," Randolf said.

Tom was walking toward his friends when he felt a twinge of warmth. The sensation grew, until something in his pocket was giving off a great amount of heat, and he reached inside his tunic to see what it was.

The acorns Lorimar had given him were now red-hot to the touch.

Tom gasped and tossed the cluster of oak seeds to the ground, where they began to twist and turn and burrow into the soil.

He smiled as he realized what was about to happen.

The ground started to bubble and churn as if liquid, and then something sprouted and started to grow.

"Lorimar," Tom cried happily as he watched the woman create a body from the stuff of a mighty oak tree.

Randolf, who had been walking back toward the bears' cave, came to a sudden stop, turning to see why the boy had called out. The others were staring at Tom, too.

"It's Lorimar!" he shouted to them.

She stood there, her body of bark, roots, and branches, her head bowed as her hair of rich, dark leaves bloomed upon her head.

Tom could barely contain his excitement, happy to see the quest's lost member return to them. "I'm glad you're back," he said, walking toward her.

Lorimar raised her face to him, and Tom immediately stopped. There was a look in her dark eyes . . . a look of danger.

"Lorimar?" he questioned uncertainly, as she quickly looked away from him and toward the others. Pulling her rooted feet from the ground, she approached them.

"Do you know this . . . person?" Bobby asked Percival as the tree woman drew near.

"Yeah," Percival replied. "She's one of us."

"What's wrong with her?" Tom heard Barclay ask, as he and Abbey hid behind their uncle's legs.

"I don't know," Percival answered.

Tom had come to join them, concerned that something

wasn't quite right with their friend. He watched as the forest woman turned her leafy head up to the trees, and at what lay nestled there in the thick branches above.

"We got caught in a storm," Tom explained. "We crashed in the trees, and we don't know how to get her down."

Lorimar said nothing, continuing to stare at the *Queen*.

"What's she gonna do?" Al asked, his curiosity keeping him awake for the moment. "If we can't figure out how to get it down . . ."

Lorimar squatted and plunged her long, twiglike fingers into the dark soil.

"What's she doing to the dirt?" Joey asked.

And just as the question left the bear's mouth, they all began to feel it. The ground had started to vibrate, and soon everything around them was quaking.

Tom looked around at the others, and all appeared as stunned as he was. Stinky and Smelly screamed and ran into the woods, the three bears right behind them. Percival pulled Abbey and Barclay tighter to him, while Randolf stood tensed, watching, his hand gripping the handle of his sword.

Tom felt a tug on his leg and looked down at a worried Roderick.

"What's going on, Tom?" the little animal asked. "What's she doing?"

Tom was about to tell him that he didn't know, when the trees in which the *Queen of the Sky* rested began to move.

At first, Tom thought the trees were falling down — they were moving in a way that he had never seen before. The full, green boughs were like open hands holding the *Queen* aloft, as the very muscular arms of the trees bent and flexed, gently lowering the sky ship.

The bodies of the trees moaned and cracked like the strikes of a whip as they leaned forward to set the great sky ship on the forest floor.

"Now I've seen everything," Percival said.

"That was great!" Barclay cried out.

"Thanks, Lorimar!" Abbey said as the twins and Roderick ran to inspect the vessel.

"You kids be careful," Percival said, following close behind. "First thing to do is to get those balloons patched up so we can be on our way."

The Rat Creatures and bears emerged from hiding and cautiously moved closer to the *Queen*.

Lorimar pulled her fingers from the ground, strands of root trailing from their tips as she disconnected herself from the earth. Randolf had returned to Tom's side.

"Did you see?" Tom asked, smiling.

"I did," Randolf answered. "Most impressive, Lorimar. I see the time away from us hasn't made you any less powerful."

The forest woman slowly turned toward them, and Tom was again struck by her troubled expression.

"Is . . . is everything all right, Lorimar? Did you find your people?"

"I did not," the forest woman answered grimly. "But my time away showed me just how dire our mission has become." She paused, turning to watch as Percival, the kids, and the bears removed the deflated balloons for repair. "Time is running out," she said. "We must continue the quest and find the final fragments of the Spark at once, for the power of the Nacht has grown."

Her words were like a cold winter chill blowing on the back of Tom's neck.

"It is already far later than we know."

EPILOGUE

The Red Dragon slept, held in the grip of the Nacht's growing power.

Try as he might, he could not rouse himself, and in turn, was unable to awaken his brothers and sisters to meet the dark threat of their rogue family member.

The Nacht believed that he was winning this war, striking at those who could thwart his plans. He was having some success, but not completely. The Dreaming had planned for something like this, suspecting that there might come a time when the dark of oblivion would challenge the light of purity and life.

And with these suspicions, seeds were planted, seeds that if proven necessary would grow into a means of perhaps stopping the expanding darkness.

The Red Dragon himself had planted one of these seeds, foolishly never believing that it would come to this.

But it had.

And now, with the help of the Dreaming, he reached out through the ether to awaken what he had planted . . . what he had hidden away, at the Dreaming's request.

The magics that kept him in slumber were strong, but he still managed to reach out to the ones who had been told to wait, to be ready if the time came.

The last thought the Red Dragon had, before fitful sleep claimed him once more, was that there was still a chance for this nightmare to be extinguished.

The spark of a chance.

For from a spark, there often came fire.

END OF BOOK TWO

JEFF SMITH was born and raised in the American Midwest and learned about cartooning from comic strips, comic books, and watching animated shorts on TV. After four years of drawing comic strips for The Ohio State University's student newspaper and cofounding Character Builders animation studio in 1986, Smith launched the comic book *BONE* in 1991. Between *BONE* and other comics projects, Smith spends much of his time on the international guest circuit promoting comics and the art of graphic novels. Visit him online at www.boneville.com.

TOM SNIEGOSKI is the *New York Times* bestselling author of more than two dozen novels, including The Fallen, a teen fantasy quartet that was adapted into an ABC Family Channel miniseries, and the Billy Hooten: Owlboy books. He also collaborated with Jeff Smith on *Tall Tales*. With Christopher Golden, he coauthored the OutCast series, which is in development as a film at Universal. Sniegoski was born and raised in Massachusetts, where he still lives with his wife and their French bulldog puppy. Visit him online at www.sniegoski.com.